Searching For Shona

MARGARET J. ANDERSON

BULLSEYE BOOKS · ALFRED A. KNOPF
New York

For Peter and Ann

DR. M. JERRY WEISS, Distinguished Service Professor of Communications at Jersey City State College, is the educational consultant for Bullseye Books. A past chair of the International Reading Association President's Advisory Committee on Intellectual Freedom, he travels frequently to give workshops on the use of trade books in schools.

Library of Congress Catalog Card Number: 77-17056
ISBN: 0-394-82587-X
RL: 6.3
First Bullseye Books edition: December 1989

Manufactured in the United States of America
1 2 3 4 5 6 7 8 9 10

Chapter One
❧

Marjorie Malcolm-Scott walked slowly up Willowbrae Road toward the narrow iron gate that opened into Holyrood Park in Edinburgh. It was mid-September 1939, and Britain was at war with Germany, but it wasn't thoughts of the war that were uppermost in Marjorie's mind. She was merely wondering what she could do to fill the day.

"You go off and play in the park for two hours," Mrs. Kilpatrick, the housekeeper, had said.

Marjorie didn't like being sent off like that, as if she were a small child who was always in the way. But that's how Mrs. Kilpatrick treated her. Sending her out and saying that she wanted to get the housework done, though Marjorie didn't see that there was much work to do. Most of the time there were only the two of them.

And what fun was there in going to the park all by herself? However, this was Saturday, so there would be other children there. Perhaps she would find someone to play with. Marjorie opened the gate and headed down toward a small pond where a group of children often played. Most of them were from St. Anne's Orphanage and Marjorie sometimes thought that in spite of their shabby clothes and frequent noisy squabbles, they had a better time than she did.

Today they were playing on a pile of rocks beside the pond, and Marjorie stood watching them, hoping that they would ask her to join in. But they were much too busy to notice her—and she was too shy to ask if she could play—so she sat down on a bench near them and tried to work out what their game was all about.

There was one girl in particular whom Marjorie watched—a girl of about eleven or twelve, with short fair hair and a faded red coat. She heard the others call her Shona, and although she was by no means the biggest, she seemed to be the organizer of the game. She and three boys had occupied the "castle rock" and the others were trying to take them captive and drag them off to a stronghold on the other side of the pond. A stray dog, excited by their voices, joined in the fight, and Shona yelled, "Wolves! They've trained wolves to attack us!"

They had already captured one of the boys and now had Shona surrounded and began to pull her, shrieking and resisting, toward the pond. Marjorie watched anxiously, hoping that they weren't really going to throw her in. Then one of the boys left on the rock yelled, "It's dinner time! Come on!" The children immediately forgot their game and went running off, right past the bench where Marjorie was sitting, never even glancing at her. Marjorie watched them disappear through the gate and then got up and walked slowly home.

She lived in a big stone house on Willowbrae Road with her Uncle Fergus, but he had been gone all summer. As she approached the house her feet began to drag. There would only be Mrs. Kilpatrick at home, and she was never exactly welcoming. Marjorie pushed open the heavy front door, crossed the dimly lit hall, and went through to the kitchen.

"Is that you back already?" Mrs. Kilpatrick asked, without looking up from the brass candlesticks she was polishing. "It seems like you only just went out."

Marjorie didn't bother to answer but picked up the *Daily Mail* and slumped into an armchair and opened the paper. It was dated Saturday, September 16, 1939. The war had started only two weeks ago and nothing had really happened yet, but the newspaper already made gloomy reading. Marjorie stared at a picture of some London children who were being evacuated to the country, and then threw the paper aside.

"Do you think Uncle Fergus will come home soon?" Marjorie asked Mrs. Kilpatrick.

"I shouldn't think so." said Mrs. Kilpatrick, giving a final rub to the candlestick. "Not with this war on. He'll have other things to worry about."

Marjorie sighed. Not that Uncle Fergus being at home made so very much difference. He was always busy with his own concerns. But he *had* taken her on a trip to France two summers ago, and last year to London. This summer they had gone nowhere. There was still another week before school started and Marjorie had found the holidays very long and boring.

The following Monday Mrs. Kilpatrick again sent Marjorie out to play in the park. The city schools started earlier in September than Marjorie's private school, so she knew that the park would be deserted except for young mothers pushing prams (and it was too early in the day for that) and staid old ladies and gentlemen walking their dogs or sitting on park benches, staring at the threatening headlines in their newspapers.

Marjorie had a piece of dry toast in her pocket and she planned to feed the ducks. When she had asked Mrs. Kilpatrick for bread, Mrs. Kilpatrick had told her firmly, "With a war on, there's no bread to spare for ducks. We'll be lucky if there's food for ourselves before this war is over." Marjorie was used to Mrs. Kilpatrick's gloom and didn't listen. Instead she took the toast she had left uneaten at breakfast. Throwing it in the dustbin wouldn't help the War Effort that Mrs. Kilpatrick talked about so endlessly. Besides, it wasn't the ducks' fault that there was a war on!

She reached the pond and was trying to entice the ducks with the toast, when a voice beside her said, "Can I feed them, too?"

Marjorie turned quickly and found that Shona, the girl from the orphanage, was standing beside her. She broke off a piece of toast and handed it to Shona, saying shyly, "I do like the ducks, don't you?"

"Especially the ones with the shiny green heads and blue and white collars," agreed Shona.

When the toast was finished, Shona looked curiously at Marjorie and asked, "Why aren't you in school?"

"My school doesn't start until next week."

"Lucky you!"

"Why aren't *you* in school?" Marjorie asked.

"I didn't want to go," answered Shona.

"But won't you get in trouble?"

"Not if I don't get caught," said Shona with a shrug. "I'll go back with the others when they get out of school."

"Don't you go to school in the orphanage, then?" asked Marjorie.

"Of course not," answered Shona. "We go to Preston

Street Primary like everyone else who lives around here."

"But what about the other children from the orphanage who are in your class? Won't they tell on you when you don't go to school?"

"There's only Tommy Walker and he wouldn't tell. He wouldn't dare!"

Having watched Shona scuffle and play with the boys in the park last Saturday, Marjorie thought that this was probably true. A silence fell between them, and then Shona asked, "Do you want to climb Arthur's Seat? That's what I was going to do."

Arthur's Seat was a high hill in the middle of the park, and although Marjorie spent so much time in the park, she had never climbed all the way to the top. Now that Shona suggested it, it sounded like a good idea.

It took them a long time to walk up the lower slopes, and they talked together. Marjorie found that Shona had seen her watching their game and had wondered why she didn't join in. "I thought you likely didn't want to get dirty," Shona said. Marjorie was suddenly conscious of her smartly tailored green coat and pale blue dress and white socks. Her long blond hair was neatly braided and tied with blue ribbons to match her dress. Shona's skirt hung unevenly below her shabby red coat and her socks had worked their way down inside her battered shoes.

There was no breath left for talk as they scrambled up the last rocky heights and reached the stone marker on the very top. They looked down on Edinburgh and all the countryside around it spread out below them.

"Look!" said Marjorie. "You can see the Forth Bridge and the Braid Hills and the Castle. I can see my house!"

"Where?" asked Shona.

"Behind the wall that borders the park down there. That's my street, and you can see the back of our house. The tall one there."

"That's a posh house," said Shona impressed. "Your mum and dad must be very rich."

"They were drowned six years ago when I was five," answered Marjorie shortly. "I live with Uncle Fergus and his housekeeper, Mrs. Kilpatrick."

"You mean you're an orphan, too?" Shona asked, her eyes widening. "Some people have all the luck!"

"What's so lucky about being an orphan?" asked Marjorie.

"I don't mean that. I mean having a posh house and nice clothes even if you are an orphan. You know who your parents were and you've got someone to look after you."

"But you've got lots of friends," protested Marjorie. "You always have someone to play with."

Shona shook her head and then sat down, her back against the stone base of the marker and said, "There aren't many of us older kids living at the orphanage. Most of them are younger, and it's always the wee ones that get adopted and move away. Nobody's going to come along and adopt me now. But worst of all is not knowing who I am and why I was left there. What were my mum and dad like? Who were they?"

"Don't you know anything about them?" asked Marjorie.

"Just the little that Matron's told me. My mum came from a place called Canonbie, and I have a picture of her house. Someday I'll go there and find out about myself. But come on! I'll be late if we don't go back down."

Shona jumped up, as if she hadn't a worry in the world, and they ran down the hill together. They parted on the road at the bottom, Marjorie heading toward Willowbrae Road with its tall houses surrounded by trees and prim gardens, and Shona toward the old part of town with its cobbled streets and crowded buildings and St. Anne's Orphanage.

"Will you be here tomorrow?" Marjorie asked, as they parted.

"I'll try," answered Shona.

They met three more times that week. Marjorie was greatly impressed by Shona's daring, and she knew that Shona envied her her nice clothes and the fact that she had money to spend. On Tuesday they ventured out of the park and bought sweets in the little corner shop right next to Preston Street Primary School. The shopkeeper winked at Shona and asked, "Playing truant?" Shona just grinned at him, while Marjorie blushed scarlet. Then they bought buns at the baker's and went back to the park where they shared them with the ducks.

On Wednesday Marjorie was disappointed not to find Shona, but the next morning Shona was waiting beside the iron gate near Willowbrae Road.

"Let's go back to your house and play," she suggested.

Marjorie hesitated. She knew that Mrs. Kilpatrick would think that Shona, with her shabby red coat and down-at-heel shoes, was not a suitable friend, but she could hardly tell Shona that.

"Maybe we could go later when Mrs. Kilpatrick goes shopping."

"Are you scared of her?" asked Shona scornfully.

"She doesn't like me around when she's doing her work," Marjorie explained lamely.

"We won't get in the way," said Shona, and she started off boldly down Willowbrae Road with Marjorie trailing behind.

When they entered the big front hall, Shona was obviously taken aback by the ornately carved Victorian furniture, the Oriental rug, and the dark paintings in gilt frames.

"It's as fancy as Holyrood Palace," she said in an awed whisper.

"Come on and I'll show you my room." Marjorie was still hoping that they could avoid Mrs. Kilpatrick.

Shona followed Marjorie up the thickly carpeted stairs and paused to look at the portraits, which hung on the walls of the upper landing. Marjorie hovered anxiously beside her, listening to the distant sound of Mrs. Kilpatrick's wireless down in the kitchen and the banging of pots and pans. If only she'd go out shopping.

"Who are all these people?" Shona asked.

"I think they're our ancestors who used to live here long ago. Malcolms and Scotts," answered Marjorie vaguely.

"You've got ancestors, and here's me not even knowing who my mum was," said Shona. She studied the paintings a little longer and then remarked, "Glum-looking lot, aren't they?"

Marjorie agreed. When she had first come to live with Uncle Fergus, she had been afraid to go upstairs alone, watched by so many eyes, and even now she didn't like to cross the landing except in broad daylight.

Her bedroom was at the back of the house overlooking the park and, in contrast to the other rooms, was very simply furnished. Marjorie liked it that way, but Shona was disappointed.

"You haven't got many fancy things in here," she said, looking around at the narrow bed, the bookcase, and the plain chest of drawers with a mirror hanging above it on the wall.

"I've got toys and games in the cupboard. Do you want to play something?"

"I'd rather see the rest of the house."

"I've got a bagatelle board and snakes and ladders," said Marjorie hopefully, but Shona was not to be diverted from her desire to see the other rooms.

Very quietly, Marjorie led Shona on a tour of the bedrooms and then went down to the sitting room. The sitting room, overcrowded with furniture and ornaments and photographs, was more to Shona's taste. She walked around examining everything.

"Who are these people?" she asked, looking at a photograph on the rolltop desk.

"My mother and father and Uncle Fergus," answered Marjorie.

"Your Uncle Fergus looks like his relatives up in the hall—a bit dour!"

Then Shona's attention was caught by a parade of

seven ebony elephants with ivory tusks arranged on the mantelpiece. The lead elephant was the biggest, and each succeeding elephant was smaller, so that the seventh was only about an inch high. She picked up the littlest elephant cradling it in her hand.

"What's going on in here?" asked a severe voice from the doorway, and Marjorie and Shona spun around guiltily. Shona hurriedly replaced the little elephant, while Mrs. Kilpatrick watched her with obvious distaste.

"I was just showing Shona the house," said Marjorie nervously.

"And raising dust and leaving fingerprints everywhere," scolded Mrs. Kilpatrick. "As if there wasn't enough for me to do without you making extra work. I told you to play in the park."

"We're just going," said Marjorie, and the two girls hurried out.

"You should stick up for yourself more," said Shona, once they were outside. "I wouldn't let her boss me like that."

Easier said than done, Marjorie thought to herself. Yet, she found herself wishing that she could be a little more like Shona, who obviously didn't let people push her around and only did what she felt like doing.

The next morning they stayed in the park, making a

fleet of paper boats out of an old newspaper and sailing them on the pond. When it was time to leave, Marjorie explained that she would be going back to school the next week and wouldn't be able to play any more.

"There's still Saturdays," said Shona.

But Marjorie knew that Saturdays wouldn't be the same. The other children would be there. Besides, with the start of school there would be ballet lessons and invitations to have tea with girls from school. But she didn't tell Shona this, because she had found that it made Shona angry to hear about the things that she had that Shona didn't—even a cross housekeeper and an uncle who was never home.

Chapter Two

~

That Friday afternoon two letters arrived from Uncle Fergus, one addressed to Mrs. Kilpatrick and one to Marjorie. It was quite unusual for Uncle Fergus to write to her, and when Marjorie opened the letter, she found that is wasn't even from Uncle Fergus himself, but from his secretary. She read it through twice before she took it in, and then she read the main part of the letter a third time.

"With the war situation so serious, your Uncle Fergus wrote to his cousin and her husband who live near Toronto, in Canada, and has heard from them that they are willing to have you go out there. It will be safer for you, and more exciting, than evacuating you to the country here. Fortunately, we have been able to make arrangements for you to travel with a group taking a train from Edinburgh to Glasgow on Monday, September 25, and then sailing from Glasgow to Montreal, where his cousin will meet you. I have written to Mrs. Kilpatrick giving her all the details, and she will see to everything. It will be a great relief to your uncle to know that you are safe."

Marjorie angrily crumpled up the letter and threw it in the direction of the fireplace. What right had Uncle Fergus to make all these plans without thinking about how she might feel—sending her off to Canada to get her out of the way—and not even bothering to write to her himself!

She brushed aside angry tears and went storming through to the kitchen to confront Mrs. Kilpatrick.

"I'm not going! I'm not going!" she shouted.

"Of course you are," said Mrs. Kilpatrick placidly. "And lucky you are to get away from all this. Who knows where we'll all end up."

"But I don't want to go! I don't want to stay with people I don't know."

"Your Uncle's cousin has children, and they'll be company for you," answered Mrs. Kilpatrick. "It'll be good for you to live in a family with other children."

"But I don't want to go on a boat," said Marjorie with another burst of tears. "I get sick on boats."

Marjorie had been miserably frightened and seasick the time Uncle Fergus had taken her to France, and that had only been a few hours on the English Channel. This would be days on the Atlantic. And although Marjorie had mostly closed her ears to talk of the war, she did know that there might be Germans out on the Atlantic, waiting to sink the boat. Somewhere in the back of her mind was the memory of the day that her parents' sailboat had overturned and the currents had swept them out to sea. She tried to forget that day, but sometimes it all came back to her in her dreams, and she herself would be struggling in the sea, unable to swim, and awaken to find herself in a tangle of blankets in her bed. The idea of spending days and nights on a boat—actually sleeping on a boat—terrified her.

"Please don't make me go!" Marjorie begged. "I'll be safe here. Other children don't have to go to Canada. They get to stay here—I saw a picture in the paper of children from London going to the country."

"They're just not so lucky as you. Not everyone has cousins in Canada who'll give them a home," said Mrs. Kilpatrick. She was not an imaginative woman, and ignoring Majorie's panic, she went about doing the packing in her methodical way.

"Your Uncle didn't give us much warning," she complained. "Here it is Friday, and he expects me to have everything ready by Monday. It's lucky you already have a passport, because you'll need that."

She found Marjorie's passport in the desk drawer and said, "Dear me! I hope they believe that this is you at the customs office. You've really changed these last two years!"

Marjorie looked at the small, nondescript unsmiling face staring back from the picture. It was a poor picture, slightly blurred, and her hair was short instead of in braids as she wore it now. Marjorie thought that there was a chance that the customs officer would not let her pass, that he might think that she was traveling on someone else's passport. She felt suddenly hopeful but then decided it was unlikely that he would hold up the whole group over one blurry picture.

And then a new worry plagued her. Suppose she arrived in Canada and there was no one to meet her. She didn't know this cousin, and the cousin didn't know her. There would be hundreds of children on the boat. How would they find each other? Suppose Uncle Fergus's cousin didn't really want her to come and didn't even bother to meet the boat. . . .

During the day, Marjorie knew that her fears were exaggerated yet at night they invaded her dreams, and she tossed and turned, afraid to sleep and unable to stay awake. The nights were long and restless, but the days went by all too fast.

On the morning of Monday, September 25, Mrs. Kilpatrick took Marjorie and her luggage by taxi to Waverley Station. The station was the scene of utter chaos. Several different schools were being evacuated, not to Canada like Marjorie, but to small towns in the south of Scotland. Mrs. Kilpatrick gave Marjorie into the care of a tall, severe lady, who checked various lists and tickets and finally pinned a label and armband to Marjorie's coat and told her to wait beside a pile of luggage. A number of other somber-looking children and their tearful parents stood there, waiting until it was time to board the train.

Mrs. Kilpatrick hung around uncertainly, feeling that she should wait and see Marjorie safely on her way, but Marjorie was so sullen and unhappy that they had nothing to say to one another. It was hard to tell how long the wait would be. Mrs. Kilpatrick's bunions were beginning to hurt and she was dying for a cup of tea.

"Do you want me to stay, my dear?" she asked.

"I don't care," answered Marjorie with a shrug.

"Well, I'll be running along then." Mrs. Kilpatrick fumbled in her handbag and pulled out half a crown and gave it to Marjorie. "Here, my dear! But don't spend it on sweeties before you get on the boat. They might make you sick."

It was an unnecessary remark, because Marjorie was feeling sick already. She accepted the money ungraciously and watched Mrs. Kilpatrick walk away without any show of emotion. Then, suddenly, Marjorie wanted to call her back. She didn't want to be left completely alone among all these strangers. But Mrs. Kilpatrick was swallowed up by another tide of children who came tumbling down the long flight of steps leading into the station. They carried their belongings in small suitcases and paper carrier bags, and they all had gas masks slung across their shoulders so that, at a glance, they looked like tourists with cameras.

One of the children waved to Marjorie, and she found herself again face to face with Shona.

"Where are you goin'?" Shona asked, setting down the small cardboard suitcase she was carrying. She wore her name, SHONA McINNES, on a large label pinned to her coat.

"Canada," said Marjorie mournfully.

"Ooh! Aren't you lucky!" said Shona. "Are all these people going too?"

"Just the children," said Marjorie. "But I don't know any of them. Where are you going?"

"Our school is being sent to some place in the country. They haven't told us where. I wish I was going to Canada, though. Do you go in a boat?"

Marjorie nodded unhappily. "I'd rather be you, just going to the country."

"Pity we couldn't change places, then," said Shona, with a laugh.

The rest of the Preston Primary children had moved down the platform and were gathered around three harassed teachers, but there were so many children in the station that it was hard to tell where one group started and another left off. As Marjorie watched them all wandering about, an idea began to grow in her mind —a wild, exciting, impossible idea.

"I'd better go," said Shona, reaching for her battered suitcase. "I don't suppose we'll see each other for a while, but I'll look for you in the park when this old war's over."

"Just a minute," said Marjorie breathlessly. "Why don't you go to Canada instead of me? They wouldn't know."

"But don't you need papers and things?"

"Just a passport, and mine's two years old. I had short hair then. The picture's about as much like you as it is like me."

"But what would *you* do?" asked Shona.

"I'll go to the country in place of you. By the time they noticed, it would be too late to do anything."

"But they'd spot you right away," said Shona, looking at Marjorie's green coat. It wasn't the kind of coat that the children attending Preston Primary wore—too new and stylish for that.

"Not if I wore your clothes," said Marjorie. "I could keep out of the way of the teachers. Would the other girls notice? Would they tell?"

Shona looked at Marjorie, and a smile spread over her face. It really might work! And how she would like to wear that coat!

"Let's go to the ladies' room and swap clothes," said Shona, speaking quickly in case Marjorie should change her mind.

The woman in charge was still busy with her lists and tickets. Shona and Marjorie dodged behind the pile of luggage and ran to the crowded waiting room. A few minutes later, inside a rest room, they quickly undressed right down to their underwear and changed clothes. Shona's gray skirt and woolen jersey fit Marjorie quite well, but the short red coat was even shorter and tighter on Marjorie than it had been on Shona. Shona wriggled around, trying to see herself in Marjorie's pale green dress and black patent shoes.

"Where are the rest of your things?" Shona asked.

"In that pile of luggage where I was standing. They're labeled. You'll find them all right. And the woman's got my passport. Just don't forget your name! Do I look all right?"

"Except for the pigtails," said Shona, looking at her

anxiously. "They're a dead giveaway. Nobody at school has pigtails and all the girls at St. Anne's have short hair. Matron cuts it herself and always makes a mess of it."

Marjorie searched in her shoulder bag and found a red manicure set that Mrs. Kilpatrick had given to her on her birthday. Taking out the small nail scissors, she held one braid in her left hand and chopped her way through it, and then did the same to the other braid. Even Matron, who didn't have very high standards when it came to hairdressing, would have been shocked by Marjorie's ragged hair. But there was no mirror, and Marjorie simply pulled Shona's beret firmly down onto her head. Someone was hammering at the door. There was no more time.

"You'd better take this," said Marjorie, and she handed Shona the shoulder bag.

"And you'd better have my gas mask," said Shona. "It's got my name on it."

Marjorie reluctantly accepted the square cardboard box that contained the ugly, rubber mask and was immediately beset with doubts. She couldn't possibly pass herself off as Shona. And did she really want to? Did she want to be one of the children from Preston Primary School heading for some unknown town to stay with unknown people? Surely, she would be better off going to Canada where there were no gas masks, no blackout, no threat of bombs, no war.

Shona had moved ahead and was already back to the place where they had left their luggage. Running to catch up, Marjorie said breathlessly, "I don't think it will work, Shona. The teachers will know I shouldn't be there, and this Matron you spoke about, won't she spot me?"

"She's going with the wee ones from St. Anne's," answered Shona. "She's not even going to the same town. Us older ones are being evacuated with Preston Primary School, and Miss Watson, one of the teachers, is in charge. I've never had her, so you're all right there. We've got partners and mine's Anna Ray. She won't tell on you, but I promised Matron that I would look out for her."

"What do you mean—look out for her?" asked Marjorie.

"She's a bit—well—not too bright, and Matron said I was to look after her. She'll find it hard living in someone else's house. You'd better go now—they're moving."

But Marjorie had one last thought. "How will we change back?" she asked.

"I'll work that out," said Shona, giving Marjorie a push. "After the war—in Holyrood Park."

Marjorie picked up Shona's small cardboard suitcase, which was unexpectedly heavy, and walked off down the platform without looking back. She told herself that if she could just stay hidden among these school children until the next day, then the boat would sail to Canada without her. Beyond that, she wasn't going to think.

Anna Ray. Anna Ray. Marjorie scanned the labels on the children's coats, searching for the girl who was to be her partner. A small, forlorn child, with short black hair and dark eyes, was standing beside a porter's trolley. Other children were jostling for a place to sit on the trolley while they waited, but the little girl paid no attention to them. Even before Marjorie could read the label on her coat, she was sure that this must be Anna, and when she got close to her, she found that she was right.

"Anna," she said softly. "I'm going with you instead of Shona. We're going to be partners."

Anna looked at Marjorie with round, frightened eyes and then reached out and touched her red coat.

"I want Shona," she said.

"I'm going instead. You can call me Shona."

But Anna drew back, her lower lip trembled, and then she began to cry. Marjorie would have turned back to find Shona right then, had not one of the teachers in charge announced that all the children in Miss Watson's group were to board the train. Marjorie and Anna were both pushed toward the train in the noisy, excited crowd of boys and girls.

They found seats together in a very overcrowded compartment. The other children were much too excited to care that Marjorie did not belong with them, and she quickly took off her coat and folded it carefully so that the name pinned to it did not show.

The train started with a jerk, and the children responded with a wild cheer, but even before they were out of the station, it stopped again, and there was a long delay. Marjorie wondered nervously why they were waiting. Was Miss Watson checking to see that she had all the children in her group? Anna was still sobbing. The other children in the compartment paid no attention to her, and Marjorie could think of nothing comforting to say.

When the train finally started again, the children were more subdued. Some were already eating the sandwiches and bars of chocolate they had brought along to eat on the journey, and Anna brightened up a little at the prospect of food. She rubbed away her tears with the back of her hand, leaving her face streaked with dirt, and then pulled a paper bag from her pocket and took out a squashed jam sandwich.

Marjorie felt in the pockets of Shona's coat, wondering if she, too, had some lunch. Anna watched her with her round dark eyes and then said, "Shona ate hers already. Before we left."

It didn't really matter, Marjorie told herself. She wasn't in the least bit hungry. She stared out of the window, and towns, villages, fields, and farms passed in a blur. What was going to happen when they found out that she wasn't Shona? She tried to imagine how Shona was feeling, but she had the suspicion that Shona was probably quite unconcerned and would even be enjoying herself. After all, Shona had managed to miss school four days last week without being caught.

"Where is Shona?" Anna asked in a low voice, pulling at Marjorie's sleeve to attract her attention.

"We've changed places," said Marjorie. "So now I'm Shona."

The words echoed in Marjorie's mind. She looked down at her unfamiliar clothes—the unpressed gray skirt, the matted jersey, the faded red coat folded over her lap so that the ripped lining was exposed. Did these make her Shona?

"Matron said Shona had to stay with me," Anna said in her small, persistent voice.

"I'll stay with you," promised Marjorie, and Anna gave her a watery smile.

When it began to get dark outside, a conductor came along snapping down the window blinds, leaving the carriage lit only by the faint glow of dim blue light bulbs. The faces of the other children stood out as pale ovals, and everything else merged into darkness.

Then the train stopped at a small station, and Marjorie heard a porter call out in a singsong voice, "Canonbie, Canonbie! Everybody for Canonbie!" Where had she heard that name recently, Marjorie wondered. Before she could place it, Miss Watson came along telling them in an agitated voice that this was their stop.

There was a mad scramble for coats and suitcases. Anna began to cry because she had lost her gas mask and wouldn't get out of the train without it. All the other children had climbed down onto the platform, and Marjorie was panic-stricken in case the train started before they got out. She groped under the seat and at last felt the square box and pulled it out, handing it to Anna.

"Put the strap over your shoulder and hurry up!" she said. "We don't want to be left behind."

The station, like the train, was lit only by the eerie blue light bulbs, giving the place an unreal, dreamlike quality. Even the boldest boys crowded around Miss Watson, intimidated by the strangeness of their surroundings.

They were led down the street to a bare church hall

where a square woman with a deep voice told them she was Mrs. Brown, the billeting officer, and that she would assign them to their families. She gestured toward a crowd of people, standing around drinking tea from thick white cups, who had watched them come in.

All this time Anna was holding Marjorie's hand tightly. Marjorie looked down at her and saw that her nose was running and that her face was streaked with tears. The pocket of her coat was torn and her shoe lace untied. Had there been a mirror in the hall, Marjorie would have seen that she did not look much better herself. Her too-small coat made her appear gawky and overgrown, and her hair stuck out from under her beret in uneven tufts.

"Shona McInnes," Mrs. Brown's voice boomed out.

Marjorie walked shakily forward, Anna still clinging tightly to her hand.

"Is this your sister?" the billeting officer asked.

"No, ma'am," whispered Marjorie.

"Only sisters and brothers can request a home together—not friends."

"Shona was to look out for me," Anna said, starting to cry again. "Matron said Shona was to stay with me."

"Oh, you're from the orphanage," said the woman, running her pencil down the list. "What's your name?"

"Anna Ray."

"We'll send you both to the Miss Campbells then." She raised her voice and shouted, "Miss Campbell, I've got two little girls here for you—if you'll just come over to this table and sign the papers."

A small, thin lady with brown hair and round glasses came forward to the table and looked at the two girls cautiously. Anna had stopped crying and looked timidly up at Miss Campbell.

"My sister . . . my sister said not to get girls who wouldn't be old enough to do for themselves. We're often busy . . . with the shop, you know." Miss Campbell spoke in a nervous, apologetic voice, rather as if she didn't expect Mrs. Brown to listen to her and that is, in fact, what happened.

"We can't all have exactly what we want, not with a war on," said Mrs. Brown brusquely, and pushed forward some papers for Miss Campbell to sign. With one last nervous glance at Anna, Miss Campbell wrote her name and then told the girls to come along with her.

"Is this all you brought?" she asked, looking at their small suitcases.

"Yes, Miss Campbell," said Marjorie.

"I'll take yours," said Miss Campbell, reaching for Anna's case.

It was very dark outside. Apparently the blackout in Canonbie was strictly enforced because no lights showed anywhere. Miss Campbell switched on a small flash-light and the girls stayed close beside her, trying to walk in the dancing pool of light that shone dimly ahead of them. At last, they turned in at a small gate and Marjorie stumbled over a step.

"We'll go into the kitchen and I'll get you a bite to eat," said Miss Campbell, ushering the girls inside. "My sister is still at the shop—all these new regulations and forms to sign with the war."

She raked the fire to life and put on a kettle and then set the table, all the time talking nervously. Luckily, she did not seem to expect an answer because Anna was too shy to speak and Marjorie too preoccupied.

When tea was ready, she told the girls to pull up chairs to the table. Anna ate hungrily, but Marjorie was unable to swallow anything.

"Oh, dear!" said Miss Campbell, shaking her head. "I hope you're not a picky eater. My sister doesn't like picky eaters."

"I'm just too tired to eat," mumbled Marjorie.

Glancing at the clock, Miss Campbell said, "It might be a good idea for you to have a quick bath and get to bed. You can meet my sister in the morning when you're cleaned up a bit."

Then she added hesitantly, as if she couldn't quite believe that their grubbiness had all been accumulated in only a few hours' train journey, "They did have baths in that place where you lived, did they?"

"Of course," said Marjorie, and then stopped abruptly when Anna broke in, saying, "You weren't there!"

"I'll show you up to your room," said Miss Campbell, not understanding Anna's remark. "I'll help you with your bath—we can't use too much water, you know."

Miss Campbell led Anna and Marjorie upstairs to a large front room. There were two single beds, and the thick blackout curtains were firmly in place.

"You find your nighties while I run your bath."

Marjorie laid Shona's suitcase on the bed and opened it, looking with dismay at the meager assortment of clothes that were now hers. She had never set much store by clothes, but then she had never thought that there were girls whose entire wardrobe consisted of three jerseys, two skirts, a ragged change of underwear, an extra pair of socks, and a short flannel nightgown.

However, there was something else in the suitcase.

Taking up the whole bottom of the case was a painting in a narrow wooden frame. Marjorie was puzzled that Shona, who had so few possessions, would bring a painting along with her. She lifted it out of the suitcase and carried it over directly under the light so that she could see it better. It showed a Victorian house, rather ornate and turreted, standing in the middle of an overgrown garden. The windows were blank and empty and, in the foreground, iron gates hung open, bent and rusted. The big stone gateposts leaned at drunken angles, and a decorative stone ball had fallen from the top of one. It lay among the weeds, chipped and shadowed, so that it looked like a skull.

Marjorie stared at the picture, and Anna, who had crept up beside her, said, "That's Shona's! It's Shona's house. She's going to find it some day."

Of course! Shona had mentioned a painting that very first day they had talked together in the park. What was it that she had said? That it held a clue to her past. And then Marjorie remembered where she had heard the name Canonbie before. It was where Shona's mother came from—the place that Shona was some day going to find.

Poor Shona! She would never have changed places with Marjorie had she known that they were being sent to Canonbie. Marjorie felt guiltier about that than about cheating Uncle Fergus and Mrs. Kilpatrick.

Then they heard Miss Campbell's footsteps coming from the bathroom. Marjorie hurriedly pushed the picture under the bed.

Chapter Three

❧

Marjorie was awakened the next morning by a light tap at the bedroom door and a voice saying, "It's time to get ready for school!"

For a brief moment she thought she was at home on Willowbrae Road and that it was Mrs. Kilpatrick's voice, and then the events of the day before flooded her mind. What had possessed her to do such a terrible thing? What would happen when she turned up at school today, saying that she was Shona McInnes, when most of the other evacuee children knew that she wasn't? Could she tell them about the switch, as she had told Anna? They would probably just tell the teacher and then there would be a terrible row. The teacher would phone Mrs. Kilpatrick and maybe even Uncle Fergus, and Marjorie couldn't imagine what would happen then. She shrank farther down under the covers at the very thought of the commotion it was all going to cause.

How was Shona managing, Marjorie wondered. At least *she* was among complete strangers, so had less chance of being discovered. But Marjorie had the feeling that Shona would be able to cope with any situation she found herself in. Other children would always be on her side.

A muffled sound told her that Anna was awake. Reluctantly, Marjorie climbed out of bed. The uncarpeted floor was cold on her feet as she felt her way across the room to open the thick blackout curtains. When she drew them back, she saw that Anna was lying huddled on her bed, crying.

"I don't want to go to school," she said.

"Neither do I," said Marjorie. "But we have to."

"Shona didn't—she played in the park. She was going to take me with her this week."

"But we don't know where any parks are around here," said Marjorie.

"Shona would have found one," said Anna with a sniff.

Marjorie turned away and opened Shona's little suitcase and pulled out a faded tartan skirt and a much-washed yellow jersey. With a pang of regret, she remembered her own tartan kilt, the pleats carefully pressed by Mrs. Kilpatrick, and the white silk blouse she always wore with it. Anna finally crawled out of bed and pulled on the same blue skirt and jersey that she had worn the day before.

Marjorie paused in front of the mirror to brush her hair and stared in dismay at the short, ragged haircut. Perhaps she could go to a hairdresser and get it properly trimmed with the half crown that Mrs. Kilpatrick gave her, and then she remembered that it was in the pocket of her green coat and that Shona had it. At that moment all her worries about crossing the Atlantic in a boat seemed nothing compared to the problems of pretending to be Shona and wearing old clothes and not having money to spend. She sat down on the edge of her bed and began to cry.

"Don't!" said Anna. She crossed the room and timidly patted Marjorie's arm. "Shona never cried. Not about anything."

"But I'm not Shona!" sobbed Marjorie. "And I don't want to be Shona."

"Come along, girls!" Miss Campbell's voice sounded impatient. "Breakfast is waiting, and you don't want to be late on your first day of school."

For perhaps the first time in her life, Anna was in charge. She urged Marjorie to hurry, and the girls went downstairs together, and through to the kitchen where the two Miss Campbells were waiting for them, sitting at opposite ends of the table. Marjorie and Anna stared at them in surprise—two middle-aged ladies, wearing identical brown tweed suits with square, padded shoulders and pink silk scarves tucked in at their necks. Their short brown hair was waved in just the same way, and they peered at the girls through round glasses.

"So you're our evacuee children," said one of the Miss Campbells, and then, turning to the other, she added sharply, "I thought I told you to get older girls who could look after themselves while we are at the shop."

"They didn't let us choose," said the second sister, blinking nervously. "And Shona will look after Anna— they're used to each other."

"I should have gone down to the church hall myself," said the first sister with a resigned sigh.

The thought crossed Marjorie's mind that the Miss Campbells probably wouldn't have to look after them for very long. Before the end of the day someone was bound to discover that she wasn't Shona, and she would be sent back to Mrs. Kilpatrick in Edinburgh, and they would have to find a new partner for Anna.

"Sit down and have some breakfast, girls," said one of the Miss Campbells quietly.

Anna began to eat eagerly, while Marjorie forced herself to swallow a few spoonfuls of lukewarm porridge. She was remembering that the Miss Campbell they had met last night had said that her sister didn't like picky eaters. While she ate, she looked from one to the other and decided that although they looked exactly alike it wouldn't be hard to learn to tell them apart. One spoke hesitantly, blinking nervously, while the other sounded much bossier. Somehow it comforted Marjorie to know that there were two quite different people hiding behind those faces and clothes that were exactly alike.

"So Agnes didn't tell you that we are twins," said Miss Campbell, noticing Marjorie comparing them. "I'm Morag, and my sister is Agnes, though most people just call us Miss Campbell because they can't tell us apart."

They hide behind their names, too, yet they are separate people, thought Marjorie.

When breakfast was over, the Miss Campbells cleared the table. Then they pulled on matching gloves and picked up identical umbrellas and handbags from the hall stand and were ready to take the girls to school. They walked back up the same road they had followed the night before. This morning Marjorie could see that the Miss Campbells lived on a street of prosperous-looking houses, all with neat front lawns behind low walls or privet hedges.

The road joined Canonbie High Street, and they walked past the church hall and the end of Station Road. On the corner of Station Road and High Street, one of the Miss Campbells stopped at a narrow little shop with a window full of dowdy hats. Above the door, in faded gold lettering, Marjorie read, "M. & A. Campbell. High Fashion Ladies' Clothes."

"I have to open up the shop," said Miss Morag. "My sister will take you to school."

Marjorie was rather relieved because she felt less conspicuous with only one sister walking beside them.

It was not much farther—only a little way down the street, but when they reached the school gate, the other Miss Campbell said, "Now, you'll be able to find your way back to the shop after school, will you? Or do you want me to meet you?"

"We'll manage all right," Marjorie assured her. Taking Anna's hand to comfort herself as much as Anna, she walked into the playground, which was swarming with children.

It was easy to tell the local Canonbie children because they were all running about, playing noisily, while the new Edinburgh children stood quietly in a group near a closed door. As Marjorie and Anna walked across the playground to join them, a bell rang and the door was opened by a tall, gaunt man. He wore a black gown and his slightly hunched shoulders and hooked nose made him look remarkably like a great, black crow.

"I'm Mr. James, your headmaster," he said. "I want all the new children to follow me to the hall after you have hung up your coats in the cloakroom. The rest of you go quietly to your classrooms."

When they reached the hall, Mr. James made a speech telling them all how much the Canonbie Primary School children welcomed them and how he hoped they would feel at home here. Then he said that when he called their names one of the older girls, Isobel McKay, would show them the way to their classrooms.

Shona McInnes was one of the first names to be called, for she was in the top class, and Marjorie gave Anna a quick smile as they parted.

"I'll find you at lunchtime," she whispered.

There were five evacuees in the top class—three boys and another girl and Marjorie. As they walked down the corridor to the last door, one of the boys stepped on the back of Marjorie's shoe, and she turned around quickly to find herself facing a big boy with curly red hair and so many orange freckles that they ran together like smudges.

"What's the game?" he whispered.

"I don't know what you mean," said Marjorie.

"You're not Shona McInnes any more than I am."

"I am so," said Marjorie.

They reached the classroom door, saving her from further questions. She had spent a lot of time thinking about what she would say when someone accused her of not being Shona, and she certainly hadn't intended to lie about it, but there hadn't been time for a long explanation, and the boy had caught her off guard.

Marjorie was relieved to see that their teacher, Miss Dunlop, was young and quite pretty. She didn't even look like a teacher. She made another little speech, telling them once again how much the Canonbie children welcomed them. Meanwhile the Canonbie children stared at them with suspicion, belying all the kind things that Miss Dunlop was saying.

Before they were allowed to take their places in the empty seats in the front row, Miss Dunlop said that she wanted them to say their names and tell a little about themselves. She asked one of the boys to begin.

"I'm Jimmy Davidson."

"Yes," prompted Miss Dunlop. "Where are you from?"

"Edinburgh, miss."

"Yes, and a little more about yourself and your family?"

"I've got five brothers and sisters and my dad's going off to the army."

Next was the red-haired boy, and he introduced himself as Douglas Craik. His dad owned a newspaper and tobacco shop in Edinburgh, and his mother worked at the picture house there so that he got in free every Saturday afternoon. The Canonbie children were impressed by Douglas Craik.

Next came a thin, pale boy, who looked younger than the others in the class.

"I'm Tommy Walker," he whispered. "I'm from St. Anne's."

"Could you tell us more about St. Anne's?"

"It's the orphanage," whispered Tommy.

"Oh, I see," said Miss Dunlop, and hurried on to the next girl.

"Elsie Walters," said the girl brightly. "I've got two little sisters and two little brothers and my dad's joined up and mum's been evacuated with the babies, but not to the same place as here, but maybe I'll get to go there, too."

While the children tried to sort out this information, Miss Dunlop smiled encouragingly to Marjorie.

"I'm Shona McInnes."

"A little louder, please," said Miss Dunlop.

"I'm Shona McInnes," said Marjorie again. "And I'm from St. Anne's Orphanage, too."

"You and Tommy must know each other well," said Miss Dunlop, and for a moment Marjorie thought Tommy was going to say something, but he only ducked his head in a shy way that he had.

When lunchtime came, Miss Dunlop told Isobel Mc-Kay to take Elsie and Shona to the dining room where school lunches were served. The girls sat on one side of the room and the boys on the other, so Marjorie had no trouble avoiding Douglas Craik. She did not, however, enjoy her lunch. In spite of a rule that they had to eat everything on their plates, Marjorie left most of her food untouched. Elsie Walters obligingly bolted down Marjorie's jam tart and custard as well as her own.

Then they all went out into the playground where Marjorie immediately spotted Anna, standing by herself near the bicycle shed, and ran over to join her. But Douglas Craik got there first and snatched Anna's woolen hat and waved it about just out of Anna's reach.

"Make him give it back to me!" said Anna.

Marjorie made an ineffective grab at the hat as Douglas dangled it in front of her for a minute and then tossed it to another boy.

"Shona would have got it back for me," said Anna tearfully, watching her red wool hat as it was thrown and kicked around the playground.

"Who is she, anyway?" Douglas asked Anna, forgetting the hat for a moment.

Anna hung her head and didn't say anything, and Marjorie didn't know how to explain who she was to this rough, bullying boy.

"She's not Shona McInnes," said Douglas loudly. "I'll tell you who she is! She's a German spy!"

Some of the children near them heard Douglas, and they gathered around, curious to find out what was going on.

"That girl wasn't at our school in Edinburgh. She's really a German spy," Douglas told them.

"German spy! German spy!" The children began to shout in taunting voices, and suddenly Marjorie was surrounded by a crowd of jeering, hostile children. She looked at the ring of cold faces and mean eyes, and they seemed to waver and blur in front of her. The sound of their chanting voices became unbearably loud, and then faded, and then became loud again. Her head began to spin and her knees buckled. She collapsed on the ground in a faint, and the children stared at her crumpled form in dismay, their voices suddenly stilled.

Miss Dunlop, who had seen and heard much of what had happened, came running across the playground and pushed between the children. She picked Marjorie up and carried her inside to the staffroom, leaving the playground unnaturally quiet. Many of the boys and girls didn't know what had happened, and those who had been part of it didn't want to talk about it.

When Marjorie came to, she heard Miss Dunlop saying to Mrs. Gray, another teacher, "They were all around her, taunting her, calling her a German spy. Our own Canonbie children and some of the evacuees. What made them do it?" And then she dropped her voice and added, "What makes it worse is that the poor child is from the orphanage, and we treated her like that."

Marjorie opened her eyes, and Miss Dunlop was immediately at her side, urging her to drink a cup of hot, sweet tea.

"Drink this," she said. "You'll feel better."

"I'm not Shona McInnes," whispered Marjorie. "I was meant to go to Canada, not here."

"Hush, now, Shona. They didn't mean that nonsense," said Miss Dunlop, and added to the other teacher, "They've even got her doubting herself."

"It was more likely that kind of talk that started it," said Mrs. Gray disapprovingly.

"I just can't think what started this German spy business," said Miss Dunlop. "But there will be no more of it. I intend to see to it that no more teasing and bullying take place in Canonbie School."

"The war has unsettled them," said Mrs. Gray. She and Miss Dunlop started talking together while Marjorie sipped her tea. She wanted to confide in Miss Dunlop—to get it all over with—yet she had already tried, and now she didn't know how to break into their conversation.

Suddenly a bell rang, summoning the children back to their classes, and Miss Dunlop turned back to Marjorie and asked, "Who are you staying with, Shona?"

"The Miss Campbells."

"The Miss Campbells," repeated Miss Dunlop with a slight smile. "Would you like to go back there this afternoon?"

"I'd rather just stay here," said Marjorie, hoping that she could spend the afternoon in the quiet peace of the teachers' room.

Miss Dunlop answered cheerfully, "That's a brave girl! We'll go right in and face them."

So Marjorie found herself back in the classroom. Miss Dunlop made no reference to the incident on the playground—at least, not in Marjorie's presence—and the children seemed to forget it quickly, too.

Even the Edinburgh children, who had known Shona McInnes, seemed to accept the new Shona as just another of the many puzzling and bewildering changes that had taken place in their lives. Only Douglas Craik continued to harass Marjorie, but he did it quietly, enjoying his power over her and Anna. In fact, it led him into a sort of petty blackmail, where he was able to extort an apple or bar of chocolate in payment for his silence.

Chapter Four

❧

The next few weeks were a strange and troubling time for Marjorie. It wasn't the fear of being found out that worried her now so much as the ease with which she was accepted as Shona. One day in October she was issued with a blue identity card, made out to Shona McInnes, and later a ration book. Sometimes she thought that even if she told the Miss Campbells or Miss Dunlop that she was really Marjorie Malcolm-Scott, they wouldn't believe her. After all, hadn't the Government given her a special identity card saying that she was now Shona McInnes, number SOCC-6-3? To Marjorie that card and number made the rash change in Waverley Station terribly official and complete.

But at the same time she was troubled by the fact that she hadn't really become Shona McInnes at all. She had Shona's name, her clothes, and her painting hidden under the bed, but she was still the lonely, rather uncertain Marjorie Malcolm-Scott. She knew that. Anna would say, at least once a day, "Shona didn't do that," or,

"Shona would have done this." And since the German spy episode on the first day of school, Marjorie had been uncomfortable with the Canonbie children. She was a long way from being the bold, self-confident leader that Shona was.

However, Marjorie was not unhappy. She enjoyed living with the Miss Campbells. Miss Morag was bossy and Miss Agnes was fussy, but underneath both were kindly souls. They provided the girls with a few much-needed clothes from their shop and taught them to knit so that they could make khaki scarves and squares for blankets for the soldiers. Like Mrs. Kilpatrick, the Miss Campbells were very conscious of the War Effort. Anna and Marjorie were *their* War Effort.

They expected Marjorie to help around the house, and she liked that. Mrs. Kilpatrick had always complained that she was in the way when she did anything in the kitchen.

"It's time you learned to cook," said Miss Morag one day, getting out a big, well-worn recipe book. "We'll start with scones. I don't suppose they let you do any cooking in the orphanage."

"No, they didn't," said Marjorie. "Cook was always too busy to have us underfoot."

Marjorie had somehow managed to fuse the experiences of her own past life with Mrs. Kilpatrick and the bits and pieces of information she learned from Anna about the orphanage so that she answered Miss Campbell's questions without any hesitation. At first she had felt a little guilty talking about St. Anne's, but now it was almost as if she *had* lived there.

Marjorie weighed out the flour and lard for the scones and measured the milk under Miss Morag's watchful eye. She let Anna mix the ingredients and cut the round scones into segments.

Anna would have liked to learn to cook as well, but she could not read the recipe book. Even the numbers on the scale they used for weighing the ingredients confused her. Anna was nine, but she had been put back to Primary One at school because of her reading. "The baby class," she called it, angrily. She had trouble with writing, too. She kept getting her letters backwards. Marjorie had noticed that Anna's printing often came out like mirror writing, and she thought it rather clever, but Anna's teacher wasn't impressed. She scolded Anna, telling her to start over again, and Anna became more and more discouraged.

Marjorie, on the other hand, was doing well at school. In March all the children in the top class would sit the Qualifying Exam, and Marjorie knew that Miss Dunlop expected her to do well in the exam—well enough to be selected to go to Nettleton Academy the following year. But Marjorie did not really believe that she would still be in Canonbie the following year. The war would be over long before then, she told herself, and she and Shona would—somehow—have changed back.

The idea that the war would not last long was strengthened by the fact that when she arrived at school one Monday morning both Jimmy Davidson's and Douglas Craik's desks were empty. Because there had been no air raids, they had gone back to Edinburgh, along with many of the other evacuee children.

School was much better for Marjorie without Douglas Craik and his teasing and bullying, but she wished she had friends in her class. The thought of all the friends that Shona would have made nagged at her. She was always with Anna at playtime and lunchtime, and they were often referred to by the other children as "them evacuees."

One afternoon, early in December, Marjorie was helping Anna with her reading. They were alone in the house because both Miss Campbells were still at the shop.

"Tommy was Spot," Anna read haltingly.

"Think about what you read," said Marjorie.

"Tommy saw Spot," Anna corrected herself, and continued to read. With Marjorie's help, she got all the way through the book. Then Marjorie looked up at the clock and saw that it was time to start making supper. Anna set the table.

The kettle was boiling and everything was ready. Marjorie went around the table changing the places of the knives and forks. Poor Anna always got them mixed up.

"I like you better than Shona," said Anna suddenly.

"Why?" asked Marjorie, quite taken aback.

"You don't shout so much when I get muddled. And you don't get me into trouble like Shona did."

"Did Shona get you into trouble?" asked Marjorie, quite eager to hear Shona criticized. Mostly Anna talked about how brave Shona was and the exciting things that she and Shona had done together.

"Once she put salt in the sugar bowl for a joke, and when Matron got salt in her tea she was angry. Shona said I did it, and Matron believed her."

"That wasn't fair," said Marjorie. Poor Anna made enough mistakes without taking the blame for other peoples' tricks.

Then the Miss Campbells came in, their round glasses misted over with rain. They hung their tweed coats and green headscarves near the fire to dry off and propped their umbrellas in the bathtub.

"It's good to come home to the kettle boiling and the table nicely set," said Morag. "We'll have a boiled egg with our tea and some of Agnes' plum jam on our bread."

She switched on the wireless, and Marjorie and Anna were obliged to be quiet while everyone listened to the news. Marjorie hated listening to the news. She preferred not to think about the war at all, but that was hard when the Miss Campbells talked about it so much, and never, never missed the six o'clock news.

Later that evening Marjorie and Anna began to make plans for Christmas. This posed quite a problem because neither of them had any money, and they were both very anxious to give the Miss Campbells presents.

"You could draw them a picture," suggested Anna. "That's what Shona gave Matron last year. She drew a picture of a horse—ever so nice, it was."

"It wouldn't be nice if I drew it," said Marjorie sharply. "I'm not Shona, you know."

For a moment Marjorie considered giving them the picture from under the bed, and then decided that wouldn't be fair.

"Maybe we could earn some money," suggested Anna.

"Miss Dunlop sometimes gives a penny to the first to get the right answer in mental arithmetic," said Marjorie. "I'm sure I could get some pennies that way."

"But I couldn't get money that way," said Anna rather sadly.

The following Saturday, Agnes Campbell gave each of the girls a shilling, saying that they could spend the afternoon at the cinema and buy themselves chips on the way home.

"Let's not go," whispered Marjorie. "We'll save the money for presents. Two shillings will be a good start."

"What will we do instead?" asked Anna. She, more than Marjorie, hated to miss going to the pictures.

"We'll go for a walk. We'll go down the hill away from the town and find out where the road leads."

As soon as they had finished lunch, the two girls put on their coats, hats, and gloves and set off down the road. It would have been much nicer to spend the afternoon in the dark warmth of the picture house than go for a lonely walk in the country on that bleak December day, but the girls plodded on. They passed the last houses of Canonbie, and then the road became narrower, and on either side of them were empty fields. The skeletons of last year's roadside flowers stood out against the leafless hedges, and a field, recently ploughed, lay dark and empty.

Then they came to one more house, bigger than any of the other houses they had passed. They could only see parts of the roof as they approached it, because it was mostly hidden by tall trees and a high wall that surrounded the whole garden. On the gatepost, in fancy lettering, was the name, "Clairmont House." Then, seeing the house clearly between the bars of the iron gate, they gasped in surprise.

"It's Shona's house," whispered Anna.

"It does look like it," agreed Marjorie, though there was something about it that was not like the house in Shona's painting.

"It's pretty," said Anna.

That was it, Marjorie realized. The house was pretty —not sad and neglected as it was in the picture. The great stone balls rested on top of the square gateposts where they belonged. The gates were tightly shut, not hanging half open, bent and rusted. And although the garden was untidy, as most December gardens are, it was not wild and neglected. The house looked empty. The downstairs windows were shuttered, and they could see no curtains in the upstairs windows.

"Can we go in?" asked Anna.

"No, of course not," answered Marjorie.

"Shona said she would take me to her house," persisted Anna. "She said I could see her family."

"We can't go in," said Marjorie. "Besides, there's no one there. You can see that the house is closed up and empty."

"Shona said I could see her house," whined Anna.

Anna leaned against the gate, pushing her small face between the bars to get a better view of the house. The gate swung noiselessly open, and Anna, without any thought, slipped inside. Marjorie hesitated for a moment and then followed Anna up the driveway.

Chapter Five
❧

Marjorie and Anna walked up the long driveway, the gravel crunching under their feet. On one side was a dense shrubbery of dripping rhododendron and laurel bushes, and on the other a smooth lawn, sloping down to a border of trees and shrubs. The driveway divided, and they hesitated for a moment, wondering whether to approach the front or to go around the back. They decided to follow the sweep of the driveway to the front door and climbed the flight of shallow steps.

It was an imposing door. The sort of door that you would expect to be flung open by a stiff, uniformed butler. Anna reached for the big, brass doorbell, but Marjorie stopped her.

"Suppose someone comes," said Marjorie. "What will we say?"

"That we want to see Shona's house," said Anna.

Marjorie was having trouble sorting out her thoughts. She was still overwhelmed by the strange coincidence of finding the house. Even though she had remembered

Shona saying that her mother came from Canonbie and that the picture held a clue to her past, she had not believed that the house actually existed. Now, having found it, she felt she owed it to Shona to find out more. But suppose someone connected with this house *did* know about Shona, what was Marjorie to do then? Should she go on pretending that *she* was Shona?

Meantime Anna, who only wanted to see inside Shona's house, pulled the bell, and the two girls heard the faint ringing echoing in some distant part of the house. Marjorie waited anxiously and was greatly relieved when there was no sound of answering footsteps.

"Let's go round to the back door," suggested Anna.

With a little more confidence now that Marjorie was sure that the house was empty, she followed Anna around to the back. Behind the shrubbery was a walled kitchen garden, with leafless apple trees espaliered against the walls. A few brown, rotting apples still hung from their bare branches, and a greenhouse with broken panes and a sagging door added to the lonely, unkempt appearance of the winter garden.

But the garden did not interest them. They were drawn back to the house. They found that there was a cobbled courtyard behind it, surrounded by low buildings. Anna tried some of the doors, but they were all locked.

"There are so many doors!" said Anna.

"These were stables, I suppose, in the old days. And this must have been the washhouse," answered Marjorie, looking through the cobweb and dust encrusted panes of a window. "I can see washtubs and an old copper boiler."

They came to the back door of the main house and, bolder now, they tried to turn the door knob. That door, too, was locked, as they had expected. Reluctant to leave, they peered in a window. They could tell from the big, black range that this was the kitchen, and they could see a heavy sideboard—the only piece of furniture in the room—with the doors partly open and all the shelves bare, confirming that no one lived in the house.

Then the rain, which had been threatening all afternoon, began to fall in big drops.

"We're going to have to find some shelter," said Marjorie, looking anxiously at the heavy clouds. "Maybe we should go over to the greenhouse."

Anna was pushing on a little square door, quite low in the wall, and gave a sharp cry of excitement when it swung open, leaving a gaping, black hole. Marjorie stooped down and stuck her head inside, breathing in stale, sooty air.

"It's the coal cellar," she said. "It's like my house in

Edinburgh. The coalman dumps the coal in here, and the maid reaches the cellar from a door in the house. That way she doesn't have to go outside to get coal for the fires."

"Can we go in?" asked Anna.

"Of course not," said Marjorie firmly. "We can't go creeping into someone else's house."

There were times when Anna could be very stubborn and single-minded, and this proved to be one of them. Ignoring Marjorie's protests, she dropped down inside the coal cellar and quickly disappeared into the sooty darkness. Marjorie could hear the crunching sound of Anna's feet as she stumbled over small pieces of coal scattered on the floor. Then came a triumphant shout, "It's open! We *can* get in!"

Anna opened a door, letting a shaft of light shine down into the cellar, and then she stepped into a hallway.

"Hey! Wait for me!" said Marjorie. She couldn't let Anna go inside alone. Besides, she *had* to find out more about the house—she owed that to Shona.

The door through which Anna had disappeared led into a small back hall with several doors opening off it. One looked like the back door and was firmly bolted. Anna was not in any of the back rooms, and Marjorie finally found her standing in the main hall, gazing up at the curve of the staircase and a crystal chandelier hanging from the ceiling, high above her. Light filtered down from the upstairs landing windows. They tiptoed forward and opened a door into one of the front rooms. A damp, musty smell greeted them. The windows were tightly shuttered, so that all that they could see was the faint shapes of a few articles of furniture draped in dust cloths. The other downstairs rooms were also dark and empty.

"I want to go upstairs!" said Anna.

"We'd better go back outside," said Marjorie uneasily. She could hear faint creakings and unexplained noises as they stood together in the hall. Suppose someone came into the house and found them there.

"I want to see the bedrooms," said Anna, and walked boldly up the big staircase.

Anna's persistence reminded Marjorie of the day that she had taken Shona through the house on Willowbrae Road. Both houses belonged to the same Victorian era, but here the uncarpeted stairs and lack of furniture made the house and all the rooms seem unnaturally big, as if they had entered the oversize home of some great, sleeping giant. The bedrooms, too, were unfurnished, except for an occasional chest of drawers or wardrobe. Marjorie gave a start of fright when she walked into a marble bathroom and caught sight of her own reflection in a mirror. The bath, which like everything else, seemed giant size, stood high off the floor on great clawed feet.

At the back of the upstairs landing was another staircase. Marjorie guessed that, like the back stairs in her own house, this would lead from the servants' attic bedrooms on the third floor directly down to the kitchen quarters.

"Come on up!" said Anna, who seemed to thoroughly enjoy exploring the house.

"These would be the maids' rooms," said Marjorie, looking into one of the small, narrow rooms under the roof. She was trying to imagine which part of the house Shona was connected with. Had her mother, perhaps, been a servant here, sleeping in one of these little rooms, or had she belonged in the big, oversize front rooms? Somehow the emptiness and echoing stillness of all the rooms made it hard to imagine people who had lived here. There were no clues at all to tell who they were.

"Can we go into the big bedrooms again?" Anna asked when they went back down to the landing. She opened a door that they had not tried before and shouted, "There are more stairs behind this door! Come on!"

Even Marjorie forgot her uneasiness when she saw the narrow spiral staircase. It must wind up inside the turret that they had seen from the outside. There was another door at the top of the stairs, and Anna gave a gasp of delight when she pushed it open and stepped inside the room.

It was a little room, almost circular, and unlike the other rooms, this one was completely furnished. A window seat, with dark red velvet cushions followed the curved contour of the wall. The windows above it reached almost to the ceiling, so that in spite of the heavy skies and the beating rain the room seemed bright. The curtains were velvet, and the floor was covered with a richly patterned carpet. A couch with carved wooden arms and dark blue upholstery angled across the room in front of the fireplace. It was a small fireplace, tiled with blue and white Dutch tiles, and on the mantelpiece above it were two stiff toy soldiers standing beside sentry boxes. There were dead ashes in the fireplace, as if the fire had only just gone out.

A child's desk and a small chair stood near the door, and against the opposite wall was a cupboard with doors slightly ajar revealing worn books and old toys. A high, narrow pram with a canopy and a rocking cradle were arranged beside the cupboard, and there was also a small table set for tea.

Perhaps it was the child-sized furniture in contrast to the large scale of everything else in the house, or perhaps it was the added warmth of carpets and curtains, but this room contained a welcome that the other rooms lacked.

"It's Shona's room," whispered Anna. "Shona's toys."

"They're not Shona's," said Marjorie, yet she could not escape the feeling that somewhere there was a little girl waiting to come back and play with the toys.

"Shona told me about the toys," said Anna.

"What did she say about them?" asked Marjorie curiously.

"When she showed me the picture she said there was a room in her house filled with toys. She said that someday she would take me to her house and let me play with her toys. She promised."

Marjorie had a sudden picture of Shona and Anna in one of the drab, bare rooms of the orphanage, looking at the painting of Shona's house. Of course they would imagine that it would contain wonderful things—a family, a roomful of toys. But Shona must have known that it was all just make-believe, while for Anna it was real. No wonder Anna had insisted on getting inside Shona's house.

Yet it *was* real—the house, the toys.

Anna tiptoed across the room to the little table already set for tea, and taking a bear and a rather stiff china doll from the pram, she was soon engrossed in a game of her own. Marjorie went over to the cupboard and looked at the books. They were mostly fairy tales and picture books, but she found a copy of *What Katy Did*. She opened it and began to read.

At last, the fading light reminded Marjorie that it was time to go home. She jumped up, saying, "The picture show will be over, and the Miss Campbells will be wondering where we are."

"The picture show?" asked Anna, puzzled. In her excitement she had completely forgotten that they were supposed to be at the pictures.

Reluctantly they replaced the books and toys and then ran down the spiral staircase and down the narrow stairs at the back of the house. They found themselves in what Marjorie guessed must be a small butler's pantry. On one wall were shiny brass bells, each neatly labeled with a different room of the house. But the house stood empty. There was no one to ring the bells, no one to answer.

They left by the same way they had entered. But it was harder to scramble up out of the little hatch door than it had been to drop down inside. By the time they once more stood in the garden, they were very dirty and disheveled. Marjorie spent a few minutes scrubbing a streak of soot from Anna's face with her handkerchief, and then they set off home through the rain that was now falling steadily.

"You've got to promise to keep all this a secret from the Miss Campbells," Marjorie cautioned Anna. "We can't tell them about the house because they think we've been at the pictures."

When they reached home, they hung up their wet coats. Miss Agnes had socks and slippers warming by the fire for them because she was sure their feet would be cold and wet after walking all the way from the picture house in that awful rain. Her kindly fussing made Marjorie feel guilty, but she pushed the feeling aside with thoughts of the Christmas present they would buy.

"And what picture did you see, my dears?" she asked kindly.

Marjorie searched for something to say, but Anna launched into a long and detailed account of some movie she had once seen. Marjorie was not sure if Anna was trying to conceal the fact that they had been at Clairmont House or if Miss Campbell's question had merely reminded her of this movie. At any rate, the account was so long, and so detailed, that Miss Campbell soon lost the thread of it and busied herself with making tea so that it would be ready when her sister came home from the shop. By the time Anna had finished, Marjorie was sure that they were safe from any more questions about their afternoon at the pictures.

Chapter Six

The following day was taken up with church and Sunday school. The Miss Campbells were very regular church goers, sitting together in a pew near the front, wearing their matching Sunday hats and tweed coats over matching silk dresses. That Sunday there was quite a delay when they found that Marjorie's red coat (which seemed shorter and tighter each time she wore it) was streaked with dirt.

"Where have you been, child?" Miss Morag asked crossly. "It looks for all the world as if you've been playing in a coal cellar."

It was lucky that Anna chose that moment to fuss about a lost mitten and divert Miss Morag's attention, or Miss Morag would surely have noticed Marjorie's guilty look and questioned her further.

Dirty though the coat was, Marjorie had to wear it to church in the morning and Sunday school in the afternoon. Anna's coat was navy blue, so if there were telltale smudges of coal on hers, they did not show.

All that next week Anna begged Marjorie to take her back to Clairmont House, but by the time they came home from school at four o'clock, it was almost dark, so there was no chance. Marjorie knew that Anna only wanted to go back to the house so that she could play with the toys in the turret room, and the thought of stealing through the coal cellar again made Marjorie feel uncomfortable. Besides, the visit to Clairmont House had left Marjorie feeling guilty all over again about having changed places with Shona. Shona should have been the one to come to Canonbie, the one to have found Clairmont House.

They looked at Shona's picture but found that they didn't really like it now. It was the same house, they were sure of that, but somehow the picture distorted the truth. It was almost as if the person who had painted it had not liked what he saw and had tried to destroy it in his picture. Marjorie shivered and pushed the picture far back under the bed.

But Anna still nagged.

"We'll go next Saturday," Marjorie finally promised.

However, Saturday turned out to be the day of the Sunday school party. Anna and Marjorie didn't really want to go, but the evacuee children were especially invited. This was Canonbie's way of making them feel at home at Christmas. So, well scrubbed and brushed, they were escorted by the Miss Campbells to the same church hall where they had been taken when they first arrived in Canonbie.

Today the hall was bedecked with paper streamers and balloons and children ran shouting and sliding the length of it. Even Marjorie and Anna were drawn into the gaiety and rowdiness of the party. Tables sagged under the weight of sandwiches, biscuits, cakes, and shivering jellies, which parents and teachers had provided, determined that, war or no war, this was to be a Christmas the children would enjoy.

A tall tree stood in one corner, and tied to the branches were presents, each labeled with a child's name. Anna spent a long time under the tree trying to spell out the names in an effort to make sure that there were presents for her and Marjorie. After tea, Father Christmas, round and jovial in his red coat and big rubber boots, came striding into the hall and distributed the presents.

Both Anna and Marjorie received two packages each. One of Anna's contained a hat and mittens, and the other a doll wearing a red dress and a green velvet coat and bonnet. The doll even had underwear and socks and shoes that came off. Anna could hardly wait for the party to end so that she could get down to the serious business of playing with her new doll. She named it Elizabeth. Marjorie also got a hat and mittens, and her other present was a copy of *Anne of Green Gables*. Oddly enough, only the day before, Miss Dunlop had asked her if she had read it.

Then it was Christmas Eve. The girls spent a long time that day choosing gifts for the Miss Campbells. Anna wanted to get them matching presents, but Marjorie was determined that they should each have something quite different.

"That way they'll know it's their own, chosen just for them," she insisted to Anna, and Anna finally gave in.

Miss Morag brought home a Christmas tree, much smaller than the one in the church hall, and Miss Agnes produced a box of delicate Christmas ornaments and allowed the girls to hang them on the branches. Under the tree were presents waiting to be opened, and Marjorie could tell that the Miss Campbells were almost as excited as they were when they saw their names on packages wrapped by Marjorie and Anna.

The next morning the girls were awake long, long before it was light, feeling the lumpy packages in the woolen stockings that had hung limp and empty at the foot of their beds the night before.

Marjorie reached into her stocking and found an apple, an orange, and a little net bag of gold coins, which were really made of chocolate. Then she pulled out three lengths of smooth, satin hair ribbon, and she was delighted because her hair was beginning to grow again and now she could tie a bow in it. Meantime, Anna was arranging her treasures on her bed, her small, pale face alive with excitement. She, too, had an apple, an orange, and chocolate coins, and in addition, a flowered nightgown, just the right size for her doll Elizabeth.

After breakfast there were more packages to open. Anna had made each of the Miss Campbells and Marjorie a pen wiper—several circles of flannel held together with a button sewn through the middle. Marjorie had knitted a tiny scarf for Elizabeth and explained that there would be a hat to match when she got it finished.

Then Miss Morag gave each of the girls a large square box. "I'm afraid these aren't new," she cautioned them. "They belonged to us when we were girls, and I hope you'll get a chance to use them before the winter's over."

The boxes were heavy, and Marjorie began to open hers slowly, enjoying the moment of wondering what could be inside. But Anna ripped hers open and with a shout of delight pulled out ice skates. Then Marjorie had to hurry to make sure that she, too, had got skates.

And she had—shiny skates, attached to high laced black boots.

Anna jumped up and hugged the Miss Campbells while Marjorie sat very still, running her fingers along the silver blade.

"I hope you don't think they're a bit old-fashioned," Miss Agnes said to her.

"Oh, no!" said Marjorie. "I like them better because they were yours. It makes us like a real family—you keeping them all that time and then giving them to us." She wished that, like Anna, she could throw her arms around them both, but she was too shy. To hide her confusion she jumped up and ran to the window saying, "I do wish it would freeze!" But all that she could see were heavy, dark rain clouds.

"It will," Miss Agnes promised her. "We mostly get a good freeze in January or February, and then you'll see all the children going to Escrigg Pond. Those who don't have skates just slide or take turns with those who have. And the old men will be there with their curling stones. Some winters I've seen them close the shops if they think the ice may not last, so they can finish their curling match before the thaw."

Then Miss Agnes opened her present from the girls —a bright patterned silk scarf. Marjorie saw Morag watching her sister as she knotted it around her neck, and she fingered her package impatiently. From the feel of it she must know that it wasn't a scarf. She tore off the paper and gave a little cry of pleasure as she held out her present for her sister to see. It was a wooden egg cup, shaped like a little man. He had a pointed felt hat to fit over the egg to keep it warm.

During the afternoon Marjorie saw Miss Morag looking at Agnes's bright scarf, and she hoped that she was not envious. But at teatime Miss Morag said that as well as the sandwiches and Christmas cake they had planned, they would have boiled eggs. She looked pleased when she served their eggs in plain white cups and set the jaunty cap on her own little egg-cup man.

That evening, as Marjorie lay in bed, she began to wonder what Christmas had been like for Shona in Canada. It couldn't possibly have been as cozy and friendly as their day had been. She thought back to her own past Christmases with Uncle Fergus. He usually took her to the pantomime, but he never seemed to enjoy it much. And he gave her lots of presents, but he never acted excited when she opened them. Then she remembered that she had never put much thought into his presents, either. Sometimes she even left it to Mrs. Kilpatrick to buy him something, but it had always been so difficult to find anything he would like or need. How much nicer this Christmas had been with all the secrets, the planning, and the surprises.

Then her thoughts went back to Shona again—how she and Anna had found Clairmont House and that there was no way to tell Shona. Was Shona wishing that they had never changed places? She surely would if she knew that Marjorie was living in Canonbie not far from the house that was somehow tied up with her past.

But she *could* write to Shona! She could write to Marjorie Malcolm-Scott at Willowbrae Road, Edinburgh, and put "Please Forward" on the envelope. Mrs. Kilpatrick must know the address of the cousins in Canada and could send the letter on.

Marjorie climbed out of bed and felt her way across the room to make sure that the curtains were closed before she turned on the light.

"What are you doing, Shona?" Anna asked, blinking as light flooded the room.

"I'm going to write a letter to the real Shona and tell her that we've found Clairmont House."

"Don't do that," said Anna. "Maybe she'd want to come back."

"That's why I have to do it," answered Marjorie.

"Please don't! I'd much rather have *you* here," pleaded Anna.

But Marjorie sat down at the dressing table and began to write the letter on a page torn from a school exercise book. She wrote hurriedly, in case she changed her mind.

"Don't send it," begged Anna. "If you tell her about her playroom, she'll come back."

"I don't know that she can come back—not while the war's on."

"If Shona wants to, she'll come," said Anna with conviction.

Chapter Seven
~

After Christmas both Miss Campbells were busy in the shop taking inventory—counting each reel of thread, each skein of silk, and all the bolts of material they had on hand. Marjorie was left in charge of Anna, but Anna seemed to have plans of her own these days, spending long stretches of time away by herself. Marjorie scarcely noticed because she was so engrossed in *Anne of Green Gables*. The Christmas holidays passed quickly and uneventfully.

One night, just after school had started, the girls were awakened by the wail of the air-raid siren. They had heard it before, but only when it sounded on Saturday afternoons at one o'clock for practice. This time it was real, warning them that there were German planes overhead, planes loaded with bombs. Marjorie's skin prickled and she pulled the covers over her head trying to shut out the sound.

"Wake up, girls! Wake up!" Miss Campbell burst into the room and started shaking Marjorie. "There's an air raid! We have to go down to the shelter. Bring your blankets."

In great haste, tripping over her blankets, Marjorie followed the Miss Campbells down the stairs. Anna was so doped with sleep that, at first, she did not understand what was happening.

The Miss Campbells did not have a real air-raid shelter, but had decided that the safest place in their house was the broom closet under the stairs. In the event of bombs falling nearby, they would be protected from flying glass and falling bricks. The structure of the cupboard actually made it almost as safe as a shelter. They had stocked it with tins of biscuits and bottles of lemonade and candles and magazines.

But when Anna reached the closet door, she suddenly became very frightened.

"Not in there! Not in there!" she shouted.

"Come along," said Miss Morag impatiently, but Anna kicked and screamed, knocking over the mops and brushes standing near the door.

They finally had to allow Anna to sit out in the hall, and her sobs subsided somewhat. Marjorie would have liked to join her. The closet was quite large, but the lack of windows and fresh air gave Marjorie a trapped feeling. It smelled of polish and ammonia and dust, and she was sure there were spiders and earwigs lurking in the corners, but the Miss Campbells were so proud of their improvised shelter she didn't like to abandon it.

"Come in and join us, Anna," said Miss Morag quite pleasantly. "We're going to have tea and biscuits."

But Anna only started to cry again.

"Likely someone shut her up in a cupboard when she was little," Miss Agnes suggested. "Did they treat you all right in that orphanage you came from?"

"Oh, yes," answered Marjorie.

"How long did you live there?"

"It seemed like always," said Marjorie vaguely.

"And what about Anna?" asked Miss Morag.

"I don't remember."

Just then they heard the drone of the German bombers. They were used to the sound of planes passing over, even at night, but to their straining ears these German planes sounded different—a dull throbbing that rose and fell with an uneven beat, a heavy sound. The sound of planes loaded with bombs.

Anna gave another frightened cry and hurled herself into the closet, spilling Miss Campbell's tea all over the blankets. By the time they had sorted themselves out, the planes had passed over. After quite a long time the siren sounded again, but with a different note. It was the all-clear siren.

They went back to bed, only to be awakened half an hour later by another wailing siren. They got up again and went down to the shelter, but this time Miss Agnes didn't bother to make tea. Anna didn't fuss, but Marjorie could feel her shivering under her blanket—probably as much from cold as fright because she hadn't bothered to put her slippers on.

The next day in his usual unemotional tone, the news commentator said that there had been an air raid on Glasgow. Considerable damage was reported.

As the raids continued, the people in Canonbie gradually gained confidence. They no longer crawled out of bed to spend their nights in makeshift shelters. The German planes were just flying over on their way to drop bombs on the Glasgow docks. But the Miss Campbells still woke the girls up and took them downstairs. They huddled under blankets in the broom closet, drinking cups of hot, sweet tea, and then crept back up to their cold beds after the all clear, shivering and wakeful, wishing for morning.

The interrupted nights were having a bad effect on Anna. As the weeks wore on, she became more and more ill-tempered, and everything seemed to go wrong. One Friday morning they all slept in. The Miss Campbells rushed out to get the shop open by nine, leaving Marjorie and Anna to get themselves ready for school. Anna dawdled over breakfast and refused to do anything for herself.

"You tie my shoes, if you're in such a hurry," she ordered Marjorie. "And you can find my gloves too!"

"Find them yourself!" said Marjorie angrily. "And you can walk to school by yourself. I'm not waiting any longer. We're late already."

Marjorie rushed out of the house and ran all the way to school, getting there after the bell had stopped ringing. She hoped that Anna's teacher wouldn't be angry with her. At playtime Marjorie looked for Anna but did not find her.

When she reached home, Anna was there, and Marjorie asked suspiciously, "Where have you been all day?"

"Mind your own business!" shouted Anna, and she ran from the room.

The next day things were worse. In the morning Anna went into the spare bedroom and took out the big box of fragile Christmas ornaments, which were kept in a drawer in the bottom of the wardrobe. She thought it a shame that such lovely things should be hidden away in a drawer all year and only looked at for a few days at Christmas. There was one ornament in particular, a tiny silver bird, that she wanted to see again.

Each ornament nestled in paper in its own section of the box, and she slowly unwrapped them and laid them on the bed. She worked very carefully, and all might have gone well had not Miss Morag come bursting into the room and startled her. Anna jumped guiltily and knocked against the bed. Two fragile ornaments rolled off and fell to the floor with the tinkling sound of breaking glass.

Miss Campbell was very angry and banished Anna to her room, telling her never, never to touch things that did not belong to her.

At lunch Anna spilled her milk, and there were more shouts and tears. Even Marjorie sided with the Miss Campbells, saying primly that one shouldn't waste food in wartime.

In the afternoon both Miss Campbells had to go back to the shop. Saturday afternoons were usually busy, and Miss Morag asked Marjorie to see if they couldn't find something useful to do. She sounded tired and discouraged.

After they had gone, Marjorie took out the big wicker basket full of newly washed clothes waiting to be ironed. She put the flat irons in front of the fire to heat.

"Can I do some?" asked Anna.

"You just go along and play," answered Marjorie sharply.

She herself wasn't quite sure about this undertaking because she had only ironed handkerchiefs and pillow cases, and that had been under Miss Agnes' supervision. However, all went well. It was very satisfying to turn the wrinkled garments smooth and new-looking, and she liked the smell of the hot cotton and linen. She was careful to test each iron before using it on the clothes, and while she used one iron, she set the other in front of the fire to heat. She hung the ironed garments neatly on the airing rack.

At last only two dresses were left, the Miss Campbells' Sunday-best silk dresses. Marjorie knew that they would want to iron those themselves. With a feeling of great satisfaction she went off to look for her book.

Anna had been sitting in the armchair by the fire watching Marjorie. She liked the easy way the heavy iron slid over the cloth, leaving it flat and smooth. Several times she asked if she could have a turn, but Marjorie would not listen. So, when Marjorie finally left the room, Anna realized that her chance had come. She could now have the fun of ironing, and also she could make up to the Miss Campells by doing an especially good job on their Sunday dresses.

She draped one of the silk dresses over the ironing board, and taking a pot holder as she had seen Marjorie do, she lifted the iron from where it had been sitting heating in front of the grate. It was unexpectedly heavy, and she swung it over, landing it with a thump, flat on the dress.

Instead of sliding easily over the wrinkled dress the iron stuck, and there was a horrid hissing sound and curls of smoke eddied around the iron. There was also a ghastly smell of burning cloth.

"Marjorie! Marjorie! Come quick!" yelled Anna in a panic.

Marjorie burst into the room and seized the iron. The handle was hot and she burned her fingers. She grabbed the potholder from Anna and carried the iron back to the fireplace. The ironing board cover was smoldering, and she poured half a kettle of water on it to make sure that it did not burst into flames.

Then she turned on Anna.

"What did you do that for? What made you do it?" she screamed.

"I only wanted to help, and you wouldn't let me," sobbed Anna.

"And I was right, wasn't I? What will the Miss Campbells say when they come home? They'll be terribly angry. They probably won't want evacuees anymore, and we'll be sent back to the orphanage. Then they'll find out I'm not Shona, and it will all be your fault!"

Marjorie raged on, and poor Anna sat in the big chair

by the fireplace, a sad, pale, crumpled figure, too frightened even to cry.

Marjorie looked at the gaping hole in the dress and shook her head. "There's nothing we can do about it now."

Anna got up, her doll in her hand, and went out of the room. Marjorie took her seat by the fire and waited uneasily for the Miss Campbells to come home. Miss Morag would likely want to send them away and get older girls in their place, girls who didn't break and burn things.

When the Miss Campbells came home and saw the ruined dress, they were tight-lipped and angry.

"It's mine," said Miss Agnes, looking at the label.

"Anna! Anna! Will you come down here this minute," shouted Miss Morag sternly.

There was no answer.

"See if she's upstairs," Miss Morag told Marjorie.

Marjorie went up to their bedroom and it was empty. She searched the bathroom, the spare bedroom, and even the Miss Campbells' room, and then all the downstairs rooms. Anna was nowhere in the house.

"Look again," said Miss Morag. "She'll be hiding in a cupboard or a wardrobe."

Marjorie didn't think this was likely, but she went all through the house again. Then Marjorie and the Miss

Campbells looked outside. It was dark and wet, and the wind snatched away their voices as they called Anna's name. She could not possibly be hiding anywhere in the garden on such a wild night.

They went inside and wordlessly hung up their coats. Miss Morag folded away the ironing board and airing rack, and Marjorie set the table for tea. Miss Agnes sat by the fire, staring into the flames.

Then they had tea, and Anna's empty place seemed to dominate the room. They didn't even turn on the wireless because they were all straining to hear the bang of the front door that would signal Anna's return. The meal was eaten in uneasy silence.

The period of waiting stretched on, and it was now almost bedtime, yet there was still no sign of Anna. Suddenly Marjorie jumped up and ran upstairs to their bedroom. She came down again, looking perplexed and unhappy.

"Her suitcase is gone. I think she must have run away —and it's all my fault. I was so cross and angry with her."

"We've none of us been very patient with the poor wee thing," said Miss Morag. "I'm afraid we'll have to tell the police."

"We can't do that!" said Miss Agnes, looking horror-stricken. "You know what people will say. They'll be saying she ran away because we were cruel to her."

"They won't say that," protested Marjorie.

"Oh, yes, they will," said Miss Morag. "This is a terrible place for gossip, and the worse the thing you say about people, the quicker it is passed on. There've been remarks already about old spinsters like us taking it on ourselves to bring up two young girls. But we can't think about ourselves. There's Anna. We've got to have help finding her, if she's out there in the dark, before any harm comes to her."

Miss Morag went out into the hall to use the phone. When she came back, Marjorie and Miss Morag looked at her expectantly.

"They were of no help," she said angrily. "They say that most children who run away come back of their own accord, and there's no sense in going out now in the blackout. They'll keep a lookout for her in the morning. What I couldn't get through to them is that there's a little girl out there, now, in the dark . . . afraid. . . ."

Her voice trailed off in a sob.

"Maybe she *will* come back this evening," said Marjorie.

"Maybe she won't be able to find her way," said Miss Agnes in a trembly voice.

They all stayed up very late, but at last Miss Agnes said that they might as well go to bed. If they could just sleep, morning would come sooner, and then they could all go out and look for Anna. That would be better than waiting.

Marjorie fell asleep surprisingly quickly, only to be awakened by the dreaded sound of the air-raid siren. She lay rigid for a moment, waiting for a whimper from Anna's bed, because Anna often cried when the siren awakened her. Then she remembered that Anna wasn't there. Anna was outside, lost in the darkness of the night, and wherever she was, she would be hearing the awful wail of the siren.

One of the Miss Campbells came into the room, lighting her way with a small paraffin lamp.

"We're not going downstairs tonight," she told Marjorie. "I expect the planes are just passing over as they did the other nights."

"Anna will hear the sirens and be frightened," said Marjorie.

"I'd thought of that, too," said Miss Cambell. "Poor little Anna! But we'll find her in the morning—as soon as it's light."

The wailing siren stopped, and Marjorie lay waiting for the drone of the German bombers. She tried to imagine Anna listening for them, too, and wondered where she could be. Where would *she* go if she wanted to run away, she wondered.

Marjorie sat bolt upright in bed. Suddenly she knew exactly where Anna would be. The little turret room!

It hadn't been dark when she left. She would have gone there to get away from all of them and to play with the toys. Then, after it was dark, she would be afraid to come home.

Marjorie imagined her now, squeezed up on the couch with carved arms, waiting for the sound of the bombers, alone in that huge, dark house. She must go to her. It was the least she could do.

Straining her ears for any sound from the Miss Campbells' room, Marjorie pulled on her clothes. Carrying her shoes, she crept downstairs in stocking feet. She took her red coat from the big, shadowy coat stand in the hall and then felt her way to the door.

Once outside, she put her shoes on, but walked on the grass to avoid making any sound on the gravel path. She made her way to the gate and walked quickly down the road that led toward Clairmont House.

Chapter Eight

⁓

The clouds had thinned   and the
moon, not quite full, shed a glistening light on the wet
hedgerows and fields. Everything looked strange and
unreal to Marjorie, and when she heard the droning
sound of the planes overhead, the dreamlike quality of
her surroundings took on the aspects of a nightmare.

Although she knew that the people in the planes
could not possibly see her, she hid in the shadow of
the hedge, wet weeds brushing coldly against her legs.
She put her hands over her ears to shut out the throbbing engines, but the sound stayed with her, right inside
her head.

They came in waves, three waves of heavy bombers,
and then there was silence again. She forced herself to
go on until, at last, she reached Clairmont House. The
gate was slightly ajar and she squeezed inside. The house
loomed up like a huge castle with its turret and sharp
roof etched against the sky. The branches of a tree
rubbed together in the wind, and drops of rain falling
from the wet laurel bushes made a pattering sound like

the feet of little animals. Marjorie tiptoed up the driveway.

When she reached the back of the house, she saw that the coal cellar hatch was open. Now she was sure that Anna must be inside. It was so dark in there, so much darker than outside, that it took every ounce of Marjorie's courage to drop down into the cellar and feel her way across to the door. It was open, and still feeling her way, she went into the kitchen. She bumped against a door and it slammed shut. With a pounding heart, she listened to the dreadful sound echoing through the empty rooms. Did Anna hear it upstairs and was she, at this moment, crouching there terrified, wondering who was creeping through the house? It was the thought of Anna's fear that forced Marjorie to go on.

She crossed the hall and climbed the curved staircase. Silvery light from the upstairs landing windows enabled her to see her way, but she had trouble remembering which door opened into the spiral stair. Finding the right door, she climbed the stairs and then hesitated again, afraid of frightening Anna.

"Anna! Anna! It's Shona," she whispered softly. "I came to find you."

There was no answer.

For a moment Marjorie felt panic. Had she come so

far, only to find no one there? She went over to the window and pulled back the heavy velvet curtains, letting moonlight shine through the curved windows, so that she could now see the shadowy furnishings in the room. At the sound of the rattling curtain rings, something stirred on the couch, and Anna poked her head out from under a quilt and asked sleepily, "Is it time to get up already?"

Marjorie ran over to the couch, stumbling over two dolls, which were lying on the carpet, and knelt down beside Anna.

"Anna! Anna! What are you doing here?" she asked roughly.

Although she was immensely glad to have found Anna, she was, at the same time, angry to find her asleep and not overcome with fear as she had imagined her.

Anna sat up and looked around, blinking. Then, fully awake, she remembered the events of the day before and cowered back down under the quilt, asking, "Are you still angry with me?"

"Of course not," answered Marjorie. "I wouldn't have come out to look for you in the middle of the night if I was still angry. I thought you would be frightened when you heard the sirens and planes."

"I didn't hear anything," said Anna.

She had scarcely finished speaking when the wailing note of the all clear sounded, and she asked nervously, "Is that the first one or the second one?"

"It's the second one," answered Marjorie. "Can't you tell the all clear from the warning by now? The planes have gone over, but they might come back. We've got to get home before they do."

"I'm not going home," wailed Anna. "I'm going to stay here."

"Don't be silly! What about food?"

"You could stay here, too," said Anna eagerly. "We could light a fire in the fireplace—there's still some coal in the cellar, and you could do the cooking."

"But we've no money or ration books," Marjorie pointed out.

"Then you'll just have to bring me food because I'm not going back—not ever."

"Listen, Anna," said Marjorie patiently. "The Miss Campbells aren't angry any more. They like you, Anna. They were so worried when they found that you had run away that they called the police, even though they didn't want to."

Anna let the quilt slide to the floor and sat bolt upright, her eyes wide with fright. "They told the police!" she shouted. "I'm never going back!"

"They wanted the police to help them find you,"

Marjorie explained. "They were worried about you."

"The police to find me!" echoed Anna, and Marjorie saw that it was going to be more difficult than ever to persuade Anna that the Miss Campbells were her friends and that they were no longer angry about the dress.

Marjorie didn't know what to do. She could hardly drag Anna home against her will. She would have to tell the Miss Campbells where Anna was hiding and get them to come and persuade her that everything was all right. But then she thought of having to go back through the dark house and venture out again into the night alone. She couldn't do it. She could only make the journey home if Anna were with her.

"Please come, Anna," she begged.

But Anna reached over and pulled up the quilt and snuggled back down under it. Marjorie, not quite knowing what to do, climbed onto the couch and lay down beside Anna, planning to talk to her, but she could not think of the right words to say. Anna was cozily warm and the little playroom had a strangely soothing quality. Marjorie decided to wait a little longer before she renewed her arguments. They didn't have to leave right away—just so long as they were home before the Miss Campbells awoke.

From where she was lying she could see that Anna had been playing with the toys from the cupboard. The little desk was now set with the tiny china dolls' dishes, and a bear, a gollywog, and a jointed wooden Dutch doll were propped up in the wobbly pram.

Was this house really in some way connected with Shona's past, Marjorie wondered. Could these have been Shona's toys when she was a very little girl, before she went to live at the orphanage? But then Marjorie decided that the toys were too old-fashioned. They must have belonged to some other little girl long ago.

Anna had fallen asleep, and Marjorie listened to her gentle breathing. Gradually she, too, fell into an uneasy sleep full of disturbed dreams. She was wandering through the rooms of Clairmont House looking for someone, but she was not quite sure who that person was. Sometimes she thought it must be Anna, but sometimes it seemed that she was searching for a child whom she had never met.

The rooms in the house in her dream were richly furnished, and the carpet on the stairs was so thick that it was like walking in soft sand. She wanted to go faster because the child she was following had disappeared.

Now she was in one of the big front rooms, elegantly furnished with ornate couches and velvet chairs and a huge grand piano. Sunshine was streaming through an open French door. Marjorie thought that the child she was looking for must have gone outside and she ran across the room, but just as she reached the door, it slammed shut, and she awoke with a start.

She found, to her dismay, that the sun was shining through the turret windows. It was broad daylight, and the Miss Campbells would be awake and would have found that she, too, was missing. She shook Anna.

"I'm hungry," said Anna, opening her eyes and looking up at Marjorie. "I want my breakfast."

Marjorie knew at once that it would now be easier to persuade Anna to go home. Anna always liked her meals.

"The Miss Campbells will have breakfast ready," said Marjorie.

"But what will they say?" asked Anna.

"They'll be glad to see you," Marjorie promised. "They're not angry any more."

"I wish I hadn't burned the dress," whimpered Anna. "I only wanted to help."

"I know you did," said Marjorie. "We'll go home and tell them that. But we must go, or they'll be thinking that I've run away, too."

"Will they really send us away?" asked Anna.

"I'm sure they won't," said Marjorie. "I think they like having us stay with them. They were worried, not angry, when they found that you were gone."

"I need to find Elizabeth first," said Anna. "And my suitcase."

"Maybe we should tidy up a bit," suggested Marjorie and began to pick up the scattered toys and put them away in the cupboard. As she did so, a book slipped from one of the shelves and fell open on the floor. Marjorie saw the name "Jane Carruthers" written in large childish handwriting on the fly leaf. Could that be the name of the child who had owned all these toys, she wondered. But there was no time to stop and speculate. They must get home.

Marjorie finished putting away the toys and then, glancing round the room one more time, followed Anna down the stairs. The empty house was not nearly so frightening now that it was daylight, and the girls walked boldly through it.

As they were walking home, Marjorie asked curiously, "Weren't you scared in there all by yourself?"

"Oh, no!" answered Anna. "I go there quite often."

"You've been there other times—by yourself? When?"

"In the Christmas holidays. And once instead of going to school," said Anna casually.

"But what do you do there?" asked Marjorie.

"I play with the toys," said Anna, as if it were the

most natural thing in the world for her to go up to that little playroom in the vast empty house and play with these long-forgotten toys.

"But they're not yours. You really shouldn't go in there," said Marjorie severely.

Anna's lower lip trembled, and Marjorie decided that this was no time to upset her. They were nearly home and she hoped to be able to slip in quietly. But they had no sooner opened the front door than one of the Miss Campbells came running through from the kitchen.

"Agnes! Agnes! They're home!" she shouted. "Both of them."

Miss Agnes came running down the stairs, and both sisters hugged and fussed over the girls and helped them take off their coats.

"Where have you been all night?" Miss Agnes asked.

"She was in that big empty house down the road," said Marjorie.

"Clairmont House?" asked Miss Morag in astonishment. "Why on earth did you go there?"

"To play with the toys," said Anna, in her matter-of-fact way.

Marjorie hurriedly interrupted her and said that Anna had found her way inside and had taken shelter.

"Well, come through to the kitchen, and we'll make

you both a good breakfast. I've got a jar of honey saved for a special occasion. We'll have honey on our toast this morning."

At breakfast Miss Morag asked Anna how she had found her way into the house, and Anna explained that a little door was open.

"You'd think it would be all locked up," said Miss Morag. "Though I suppose there's nothing much left in there."

"Whose house was it?" asked Marjorie. She was dying to find out.

"It belonged to old Mr. Carruthers," said Miss Agnes. "He died back in the spring, and there was a big sale in the summer."

"We got the coat stand there," said Miss Morag. "It's a bit big for our hall."

"I'm afraid I was the one who bid on it," said Miss Agnes, blushing a little. "I got carried away."

"Well, at least you didn't get that awful birdcage with the stuffed parrot in it! What would we have done with that?"

Marjorie wanted to ask more about Mr. Carruthers and how the house had looked when he lived there, but Miss Morag suddenly glanced up at the clock and said, "Look at the time! We must get ready for church. What are you going to wear, Agnes?"

There was an awkward pause, and Anna looked at Miss Agnes with a woebegone expression.

"You go ahead and wear your silk dress," said Miss Agnes smoothly. "I can just wear this skirt and blouse today."

Miss Morag looked doubtful but finally went upstairs to put on her Sunday dress.

"Morag and I were talking while she was ironing her dress this morning, Anna," said Miss Agnes. "We've decided that with the war on it wouldn't be right for us both to get new dresses, so my sister will go on wearing her silk, and I'll pick out something suitable from the shop. I'm quite looking forward to choosing something of my own."

She gave a pleased little smile and leaned over and patted Anna's cheek, and Anna grinned back at her. Miss Agnes didn't feel bad about the dress at all. Both girls were suddenly sure of that.

Chapter Nine

A day or two later when Marjorie came home from school, Miss Campbell told her that there was a letter for her on the hall stand. Thinking that it must be an answer to her letter to Shona, she snatched it up and ran to her room, only to find that it was the very same letter she had written. Across the envelope was stamped, in great black letters, UNKNOWN, and in smaller letters, RETURN TO SENDER.

Looking at the envelope with the name Marjorie Malcolm-Scott partly obscured by the word UNKNOWN gave her an awful feeling. It was as if everything that she had known and done before she became Shona had never happened. As if she had no past. Mrs. Kilpatrick *had* to know where Marjorie was. Marjorie couldn't just have disappeared. And then it occurred to her that Mrs. Kilpatrick might no longer live in the house on Willowbrae Road. Uncle Fergus would surely have some important job connected with the war in London or somewhere like that. With no Marjorie for Mrs. Kilpatrick to look after, there would be nothing for her to do.

Marjorie could think of no other way of reaching Shona now. And probably Shona had no way of finding her. She wondered once again how long the war would last. Maybe for years and years. But somehow that still didn't seem likely. She heard people say that the British would beat the Germans before summer and then—somehow—she and Shona would find each other again. But the feeling that there was no Marjorie Malcolm-Scott stayed with her. She was UNKNOWN. There were now two Shonas.

Marjorie was very busy these days with school work. Miss Dunlop gave her extra lessons to help her when it came time to take the Qualifying Exam. One afternoon, when she stayed late for help on fractions, Miss Dunlop said suddenly, "I wrote to Mrs. Holmsworth, your matron at St. Anne's, to tell her how well you are doing at school."

Miss Dunlop was waving a letter in front of her, and Marjorie stiffened, sure that she had been caught at last. Miss Dunlop seemed to be waiting for her to say something, so she asked cautiously, "How could you write to her? I thought she had been evacuated, too—with the little ones."

"So she was, but I have her address and, of course, she has yours. We have to keep records, you know. We wouldn't want to misplace any of you!" said Miss Dunlop lightly. "She says it's a pity that you are billeted so far from Gatebridge where she is, because she would like to see you and Tommy and Anna again."

Marjorie's face grew hot and her heart was beating uncomfortably fast. She was sure that Miss Dunlop expected her to say something, but she did not trust her voice.

"She says that she's surprised that you are doing so well," continued Miss Dunlop, smiling. "She claims that you were good at drawing and had lots of imagination but never showed much interest in your school work, especially arithmetic. Isn't it funny how teachers can see children so differently!"

Marjorie sat very still, her hands clenched and her nails digging into her palms, waiting for the suspicious questions to begin, but Miss Dunlop tossed the letter aside and went back to correcting the pile of exercise books on her desk.

"Miss Dunlop," said Marjorie, at last. "Do you think she'll *ever* come and see us?"

"I can't really say," answered Miss Dunlop. "You know how difficult traveling is in wartime, and you've seen these posters asking, 'Is your journey really necessary?' Besides, she seems to have her hands full where she is."

Matron turning up was a threat that hadn't occurred to Marjorie. Miss Dunlop made it seem unlikely that Matron would come—but Marjorie was beginning to think that it was the unlikely things you had to watch out for.

She was no longer in the mood for fractions, and closing her book, she said, "I think I'll go home now."

Miss Dunlop looked up. "You do look a little strained, Shona. No sense in overdoing it. You run along!"

Marjorie ran most of the way home. It was very cold, and not for the first time, she wished that Shona had owned a warmer coat. The only good thing about the cold weather was the news that Escrigg Pond was already frozen over.

By Friday the ice was holding. When Anna and Marjorie arrived home from school Miss Agnes was waiting for them with extra thick socks and long woolen scarves.

"I hear they're skating on the pond today," she said, her eyes bright behind her round glasses. "How excited Morag and I used to be when we heard the ice was holding! We were always among the first down there. You'll be wanting to get down there, too, and try out those skates."

She wrapped the long scarf around Anna's neck, crossed it over her chest, and pinned it behind her back.

"There, child, that should keep out the wind," she said. "You'll find your way all right, will you? You take the first road to the left after you pass Clairmont House down to Escrigg Farm. There used to be a sign there, but I think they've taken it down—to confuse any Germans that land by parachute. A piece of nonsense, I say! What difference would it make to any spy to know that that road leads to Escrigg Farm?"

"It would if he wanted to go skating," said Anna, with a giggle.

"Anyway, take that lane and keep going right past the farm and you'll come to the pond."

Marjorie was so excited that she scarcely listened to Miss Campbell's directions. The girls set off, their skates tied together and slung over their shoulders. The air was crisp and clear, and their breath made little clouds of fog when they spoke to one another. They passed Clairmont House without giving it a glance and turned down the narrow lane to the farm. Anna jumped from one frozen puddle to the next, cracking the ice.

Long before they reached the pond, they could hear the voices of the skaters echoing in the clear air, and once they passed Escrigg Farm they could see the pond and small, dark figures weaving about on the ice. Both girls broke into a run, eager to join the lively crowd.

In the autumn the pond was used for duck hunting, and a small triangular blind had been built with a narrow wooden walkway leading out to it. Marjorie and Anna walked along this walkway past the rushes at the edge of the pond where the ice was brittle and then sat down on it to take off their shoes and put on their skates.

It took them a long time to lace the high boots, and their fingers were soon stiff with cold. Anna's lace got knotted, and Marjorie, very impatiently, helped her untangle it. At last they were ready and they stood up unsteadily. How could the other children move so effortlessly when they felt so clumsy and weighted down? Marjorie took a cautious step forward and felt the muscles in her calves and feet tighten.

"I wish there was something to hold onto," said Anna.

"Don't hold onto me," warned Marjorie.

Just then, Isobel McKay, from Marjorie's class at school, came gliding across the ice and curved to a stop beside them.

"Hello, Shona," she said. "Have you been skating before?"

If Marjorie's cheeks had not already been red from the sharp cold, she would have glowed with pleasure at the idea of Isobel coming over to speak to her, and she wished that her feet didn't feel so heavy. She pushed one foot forward and immediately lost her balance and landed with a thud on the ice.

"Put your hands on my shoulders and try moving your feet like I do," said Isobel, when Marjorie managed to struggle to her feet again.

Marjorie leaned on Isobel and gradually began to get the feel of it.

"I'm going to try by myself," said Marjorie, letting go of Isobel's shoulders. She was wobbly, yet she was surprised to find that she was managing. She would get no points for style or speed, but she *was* staying upright.

Then Billy Wallace, a boy from their class, skated past them shouting, "It's Shona Lot, Mona Lot!"

Everybody listened to the Tommy Handley Hour on the wireless and knew the whining voice of Mona Lot, so all the children thought this was very funny and took up the shout. "Shona Lot, Mona Lot!" echoed in the cold air. But this time the name calling was good-natured and made Marjorie feel that she was, at last, one of them. Two other girls offered to take her skating between them, and she was halfway around the pond before she looked back at Anna. Anna was still sitting where Marjorie had left her, but Marjorie was having too much fun to worry.

But after a while Marjorie did leave her friends and

reluctantly headed back to Anna. She went around the edge of the pond because some of the bigger boys were playing hockey out in the middle, and Marjorie did not want to skate between them.

"I'm cold," Anna complained, when Marjorie was close enough to hear. "I want to go home."

"It's because you don't keep moving. You've got to get out there and try, Anna! You won't learn sitting down."

"Every time I stand up, I *do* sit down," said Anna tearfully, but she did try to stand up again. Her ankles were bent, so that she was almost standing on the side of her skates. She took two uncertain steps.

"That's the way!" said Marjorie encouragingly.

Just then Isobel skated up to them saying, "Come on, Shona! Let's go straight across."

With an apologetic smile to Anna, Marjorie followed Isobel out onto the ice among the fast-moving hockey players. The sun had set and the moon was rising in the clear sky, giving the ice and frost-encrusted trees and grass a strange silver cast. The sounds of voices and the ring of skates on the ice seemed more melodious in the dark. Marjorie, surrounded by friends, felt as if she were in an enchanted dream.

She was not sure how long she had been skating when

she heard a shout from across the pond near the duck blind, and two of the big boys went skating over to find out what the trouble was. They came back quickly, dark shapes weaving across the ice, and scraped to a halt beside Marjorie.

"It's that little kid that stays with you," one of the boys said. "She's fallen down and hurt herself. They're taking her to Escrigg Farm."

Marjorie's knees began to wobble. Her skates seemed heavy and useless, and she longed to kick them off so that she could run across the ice and find out what had happened to Anna. Even with Isobel's help, she found it a great effort to cross the space of ice that separated her from Anna.

By the time she got there, they had already carried Anna to the farm, and no one really knew how badly she had been hurt, though there were plenty of people who were willing to talk about it.

"Cut her head open on a skate," somebody said. "You should have seen the blood."

"It's a broken leg," said someone else.

Marjorie was cold and tired and her feet were numb and her legs ached. It took her forever to unlace her boots, and then she could not find her shoes. At last she saw them, and Anna's too. She thrust her feet into her shoes, and picking up Anna's, she went running toward the farm house, desperately afraid of what she was going to find.

She pounded on the door, and it was immediately opened by a plump, rosy-cheeked woman.

"You'll be Shona," she said. "I'm Mrs. Appleby. And I'm glad to see you've brought Anna's shoes! Come on in! She's waiting for you."

"Is she all right?" asked Marjorie breathlessly.

"She's got a bit of a bump on the head, that's all. Coming up like an egg, it is, and they say it knocked her out for a spell. Dr. Knight is coming to take a look at her, and I'm sure he'll be giving you both a ride home. Come on in by the fire and see Anna for yourself."

Anna was sitting in a big stuffed chair, a rug over her knees, drinking a cup of tea. She looked remarkably well, and Marjorie thought that the rumor-spreaders down by the pond would be disappointed to see her looking so hale and hearty.

"Let me give you a cup of tea, too," said Mrs. Appleby, placing a platter of warm scones between the girls.

"It puts me in mind of the time Jane Carruthers fell through the ice," said Mrs. Appleby, when she brought Marjorie her tea. "They brought her back here, dripping wet and scared half to death, poor wee thing."

"Jane Carruthers?" whispered Marjorie.

"Aye! Maybe you've heard of her. She lived in Clairmont House—that big place you pass just before you turn down our road."

"Was that a long time ago?" asked Marjorie.

"It must be twenty years ago. It was when my girl, Becky, was the parlormaid up there. Jane had got these new skates for her birthday and couldn't wait to try them. The ice wasn't very thick, and she went through it there by the rushes where the brook runs into the pond. You want to watch that place—it's always the last to freeze over."

"Did she nearly drown?" asked Anna anxiously.

"Dear me, no!" answered Mrs. Appleby. "It's not deep, but she got an awful cold, as I remember, and Becky had to carry all her meals up to her in that little room in the tower, and the coal for the fire, as well. They overworked Becky there, and small thanks she ever got."

"What was Jane like?" Marjorie asked.

"She was a bonny wee thing with golden ringlets—like a china doll. But headstrong! It was just like her to slip out and go skating when she'd been told that she couldn't. Becky used to say she was spoiled, with all her fine clothes and toys, but I fancy she was a lonely, wee lass. Her mother died in the flu epidemic at the end of the last war, and her father never had much time for her."

"Did she have any brothers and sisters?" asked Marjorie, eager to find out all that she could about the family in Clairmont House.

"There was a brother, John, who was about ten years older than her, but he was killed in the last war. Mr. Carruthers never got over that, they say, losing first his boy and then his wife. A terrible thing! And they said that would be the war to end all wars, and here we are at it again. There's just no sense to it," said Mrs. Appleby, shaking her head.

Marjorie wanted to get the conversation back to Jane, but there was a loud knock at the door, and Dr. Knight walked in. Seeing Anna sitting there, cheerfully drinking tea and eating the last scone, he didn't waste much time examining her but offered to take the girls home. He stopped in and talked to the Miss Campbells who were, of course, greatly agitated when they heard about Anna's fall. They bustled around fixing supper for Dr. Knight and the girls. Marjorie and Anna ate with such hearty appetites that no one would have guessed that they had polished off a plate of scones at Escrigg Farm.

The next morning Marjorie said rather hesitantly to Anna, "I'm sorry you didn't have much fun skating yesterday. Today I'll stay with you more."

"Will you really?" asked Anna eagerly.

"I promise."

The Miss Campbells wanted Anna to stay home and rest, but Anna reassured them. "I won't fall down today," she said. "Shona is going to help me."

When they reached the pond, several of the children, including Isobel, were already there, and they crowded around Anna asking her about her fall and respectfully feeling the bump on her head.

"We'd better see that she doesn't knock herself out again," Isobel said to Marjorie. "You skate on one side of her and I'll go on the other."

Between them, they led Anna out onto the ice, and Marjorie was pleased to find that she was already steady enough on her skates to be able to help Anna, even when Anna wobbled. By the end of the morning, Anna was venturing out on her own and enjoying herself as much as the others.

The prolonged cold weather caused a lot of hardship, especially when food and fuel supplies began to run low. Farmers worried about their sheep and cattle, and blizzards disrupted the movement of troop trains. But for Marjorie and Anna it was a happy time. They were no longer "them evacuees" but were now Canonbie children.

Chapter Ten

It was a great disappointment to both Marjorie and Anna to awaken one morning to the sound of rain beating against the window. Marjorie drew back the heavy curtains and stared out at the thick, gray clouds.

"I wish it could have stayed cold forever," said Anna, joining her at the window.

"So do I." Marjorie agreed with her. "But I suppose we could get tired of it."

"I wouldn't," said Anna.

However, the best part of skating stayed with them. They now had friends at school, and Marjorie asked Miss Campbell that morning at breakfast if she could bring Isobel home for tea.

"I suppose so," said Miss Campbell. "But there won't be anything fancy."

Marjorie asked Isobel rather diffidently, but found that Isobel was eager to come.

"I think the Miss Campbells are ever so funny," giggled Isobel. "I've always wondered if they eat exactly the same things at the same time. 'Shall we have marmalade on our toast this morning, Miss Campbell?' 'No, Miss Campbell, I think we should have honey today!' And how do they decide what to wear? 'Shall it be the pink or the blue knickers, today?' "

Isobel doubled up with laughter at her own joke, but Marjorie wasn't sure that she liked Isobel making fun of the Miss Campbells like that. She was relieved that when Isobel came to tea she was very quiet, even shy.

After tea, when Isobel's shyness was wearing off, Marjorie suggested that they should go for a walk, and they set off down the road. It was a drizzly, gray evening, but the girls were glad to be outside.

"Do you like it here better than the orphanage?" Isobel asked suddenly. "I should think it would be a bit quiet for you with just the Miss Campbells and Anna after living with so many people."

"It's better here," said Marjorie.

"Did they make you work hard at that place where you lived before—scrub floors and all that?"

"They had maids who did the scrubbing," said Marjorie. "We went to school and played in the park just like other kids."

Marjorie had sometimes thought about confiding in Isobel, but by now she had told so many falsehoods that it was almost as if she couldn't disentangle the truth from the lies. Besides, Marjorie had the comfortable feeling that she was now accepted as Shona McInnes, the Miss Campbells' evacuee from St. Anne's, and she didn't want to change that. She was happier now than she had ever been at Willowbrae Road. She hadn't managed to capture the bold self-confidence that she was sure Shona possessed, but she had left behind some of the uncertainty and loneliness that had belonged to Marjorie. Even Anna no longer distinguished her from "the real Shona," and spoke to her as if they had shared past adventures in the orphanage.

Marjorie and Isobel had reached the gate of Clairmont House. Lately Marjorie had been so busy with skating that she had not given much thought to finding out more about the Carruthers but now seeing the house again brought back all her curiosity. She looked up at the turret windows half expecting to see the wistful face of Jane Carruthers peering out, but all the windows stared back blankly. Maybe she and Isobel could, together, discover something about the history of the house.

"I know how to get inside that house," said Marjorie. "Anna and I have been in there."

"Go on, Shona!" said Isobel, not believing her. "You didn't dare do that!"

"We did, too!"

"I know I wouldn't," said Isobel. "That house is haunted."

It was now Marjorie's turn to be skeptical. "Who by?" she asked.

"Old Mr. Carruthers! He died last year. Right in that front room. You wouldn't catch me going in there for anything."

"Do you really believe in ghosts?" asked Marjorie.

"His ghost, I do," said Isobel. "Some of us kids used to sneak in through the gate there and try to cut across the garden without him seeing us. But he'd always spot us from his window up there, and he'd shout and shake his fist. I bet his ghost is up there watching to see that we don't sneak in."

"If you used to go into his garden when he lived there, then surely you're not frightened to go in now when there's nobody there."

Isobel shook her head. "I'm not going in."

"Do you know anything about Mr. Carruthers? Or about his family?" Marjorie asked.

Again Isobel shook her head. "He never had a family," she said.

"He did so! Mrs. Appleby said he had a son called John who was killed in the last war and a daughter called Jane with golden curls."

"Not that old man," said Isobel positively. "I've never heard of him having children, and if he did they'd be grown-up. Why, I bet he was eighty years old!"

The girls turned and walked slowly home. Marjorie was disappointed that Isobel knew nothing more about the Carruthers. How was she ever going to find out how Shona had happened to own the painting of Clairmont House and what connection there was between her and the Carruthers family? She had tried asking Miss Morag, but that had reminded Morag of Anna's running away and the burned dress, and they had never got back to the subject of the Carruthers.

When they reached home it was time for Isobel to leave, and she politely thanked the Miss Campbells for having her.

"A nice child," Miss Morag pronounced. "You may ask her to come again."

A few days later the top class took the Qualifying Exam. It all seemed very important as desks were set up in the hall, spaced far apart. Marjorie was surprised to see Dr. Knight in the hall as well as Miss Dunlop and Mr. James, the headmaster.

"What's Dr. Knight doing here?" Marjorie asked Isobel. "Do they think we're going to faint when we see the questions?"

Isobel giggled. "He's here to see we don't cheat," she explained. "He always comes in for the Qualifying."

Dr. Knight gave Marjorie a friendly wink as he passed

out the papers. Then he sat down at the front of the hall, chewing on his unlit pipe, and read a book. The only sound in the hall was an occasional perplexed sigh and the shuffle of feet. Billy Wallace dropped his pencil, and all the children raised their heads from their work as he walked up to the front of the room to sharpen it.

Marjorie rather enjoyed the exam, especially the arithmetic and the intelligence test. Miss Dunlop smiled at her encouragingly when she gathered in the papers and asked her if she had found it hard.

"Not too bad," said Marjorie, and then she more or less forgot about it. Now that she was happier at Canonbie she was no longer sure that she wanted to be chosen to go to the Academy the following September. It would mean being the new girl all over again and having to make new friends.

It was now light later in the evenings, and Anna and Marjorie often went out together, exploring the countryside. The hedgerows were beginning to turn green and delicate spring flowers were blooming in the woods.

"Let's go and see Mrs. Appleby at Escrigg Farm," suggested Marjorie, as they walked down the road together one day after school.

"I want to go to Clairmont House," said Anna.

"To Clairmont House? Do you still go there?" asked Marjorie in surprise.

"Sometimes," said Anna. "There's something I want to show you."

"You shouldn't go there," scolded Marjorie. "Are you still playing with those toys?"

"I want you to read a book to me," said Anna.

"We've got books at home that I can read to you."

"Not like this book," interrupted Anna. "This isn't a real book. It's just written in pencil. I think that girl Mrs. Appleby told us about wrote it—the girl who fell through the ice."

"Jane Carruthers?" asked Marjorie.

"I saw 'Jane' in it, but most of it is too hard to read."

"Do you think that it could be a diary?" asked Marjorie, really interested now.

Anna nodded.

The idea that they could, by themselves, find out something more about the people who had once lived in Clairmont House was enough to overcome any qualms Marjorie might have had about going into the house again. She wasn't in the least frightened by Isobel's idea that the house was haunted, but she did worry about being caught trespassing, though she could not imagine who would care.

The garden looked more neglected now, with the first lush growth of spring. Daffodils nodded among the weeds in a border under the window, and bluebells were growing in the long grass at the edge of the shrubbery.

They entered the house through the coal cellar as before. Once inside, Marjorie was uneasy, struck again by the size and emptiness of the house. But when they reached the sanctuary of the little turret room, everything looked welcoming, just as it had when they first found it.

Anna ran over to the small cupboard, obviously quite familiar with its contents, sorted through a pile of books, and brought out a small, buff-colored exercise book for Marjorie to read.

They sat together on the couch in front of the empty fireplace, and Marjorie opened the book. She saw that it was filled with neat, though childish, handwriting. She turned back to the first page and read, "Jane Carruthers. My Diary. January, 1920. I have decided to write a journal, although nothing exciting ever happens."

The first few pages of the diary seemed to confirm that, indeed, nothing exciting did happen to Jane. They were a catalogue of what Jane wore each day and of what she ate. Mrs. Johnstone was mentioned once or twice, and Marjorie thought that she was, perhaps, a housekeeper or governess. Then, a few pages farther on, she came to an entry that made Marjorie and Anna feel that they were reading about a real friend of theirs.

"January 31. Escrigg Pond is frozen over and I want so badly to try out my new skates. Mrs. Johnstone says I can't go today and, of course, I can't go tomorrow because it is Sunday. By Monday, who knows, the ice may be gone. But I have a plan. I'm going to slip out this evening. What an adventure!!"

The next entry, on February 4, read: "The adventure didn't turn out at all well. I was no sooner out on the ice than—crack!—I went right through. It was very cold and I was sure I would drown. Someone from Escrigg Farm heard me screaming and rescued me and took me to the farm. Mrs. Appleby was very kind and wrapped me up in a blanket and made me tea and hot scones."

"Just like she did for me!" said Anna, her face shining. Mrs. Appleby's kindness seemed to forge a link between the girls.

"Let me read more," said Marjorie.

"Mrs. Appleby is Becky the maid's mother. It was nice at the farmhouse but it stopped being nice when Mrs. Johnstone arrived in a rage. She wasn't a bit sorry that I had nearly drowned and told Papa and he was in a rage, too. Now I have a cold and have to stay in the playroom all the time and they say it serves me right. I wish I *had* drowned, then they'd be sorry."

"Poor Jane!" said Anna. "They were horrid to her."

"Listen to this," said Marjorie, reading another entry. "Becky stayed and played with me today. We played dominoes and I won. Then I taught her to play Ludo and she won that. Games are no fun if there is no one to play with. I hope she comes again soon."

Marjorie laid down the diary and went over to the toy cupboard. She found a box of dominoes, yellow ivory ones with black dots.

"Here's the Ludo board, too. Isn't it strange to think that these are the toys she's writing about?"

"I wish she could play with us," said Anna.

"I think she would have liked that. She sounds rather lonely. But she'll be grown up by now. This was written twenty years ago."

"Read some more," said Anna.

"There isn't much more," answered Marjorie. "I suppose she got tired of keeping a diary. I usually do. But here's something about Becky again."

"May 14. I was hiding in the loft above the stable spying on Danny, the groom, when Becky came in. She and Danny whispered together and I jumped down out of the loft and scared them out of their wits! Becky was so angry that she says she will never come up and play with me again. I hope she doesn't mean it."

Marjorie turned to another page in the diary, which was written in June. "Becky and Danny are going to be married so she won't work here any more. I wish I were old enough to get married and move away from here. Mrs. Johnstone was angry today because I tore my white dress—the one with the lace on the bodice and pink flowers—and she locked me in the playroom with no supper."

Anna had climbed onto the window seat and was looking out. Suddenly she stiffened, and when she turned around, her face was white and her eyes huge.

"There's soldiers down there! Soldiers with guns! And they're coming to look for us!"

Marjorie jumped up beside Anna and saw that she was right. There were soldiers—everywhere. Several army lorries were parked in the driveway, and dozens of soldiers were jumping out of the backs of them and throwing out rifles and duffle bags. Some of them were already approaching the front door.

Anna and Marjorie, confused by the sudden appearance of the soldiers, imagined that somehow the dreaded German army had come. All the awful things they had heard about the Germans, whispered from child to child in the school playground and then pushed to the backs of their minds, suddenly confronted them. Dropping the diary, Marjorie wrenched open the door and hurtled down the spiral staircase with Anna behind her.

Soldiers were already swarming through the front door into the main hall. Great big men in khaki uniforms with rifles and huge boots. The giants the house had been waiting for.

"The back stairs," said Marjorie breathlessly, and Anna followed her. "We can get down the back stairs to the kitchen without them seeing us."

There was so much noise in the front hall that no one heard the two girls clattering down the uncarpeted stairs. They darted through the door into the darkness of the coal cellar like frightened rabbits diving into a burrow. Marjorie peered out the open hatch and could see that no one was around the back of the house. She heaved herself up, out through the hatch, and then turned and dragged Anna out.

They ran across the cobbled courtyard and made for the shrubbery. There, under the cover of the thick bushes, they crept toward the gate. Underfoot grew wild garlic, its smell so pungent that Marjorie was afraid it would attract the attention of the soldiers. For a long time afterwards, the smell of wild garlic always brought back something of the panic she had experienced that day.

They managed to duck out the open gate, unnoticed, and were walking along the road when Anna asked in a small voice, "Were they looking for us? Would they have shot us?"

Marjorie, calmer now that they had reached the safety of the road, said in a rather superior voice, "Of course not! They were British soldiers, you know. They might have been angry with us for being in there, but they wouldn't have shot us."

"What were they doing inside the house?"

"Maybe the Miss Campbells will know," Marjorie suggested. "We'll ask them. But don't *you* say anything. Let *me* do the talking."

Chapter Eleven

After the table had been cleared, the Miss Campbells and Marjorie and Anna all sat around the fire, each with their knitting. Marjorie was making a scarf and she wished, for the hundredth time, that soldiers didn't have to wear that awful khaki color. She was sure that her knitting would go faster in some other color. Why not patriotic scarves of red, white, and blue?

Anna was still knitting squares for the blanket, except that they were never quite square, because if she stopped in the middle of a row she couldn't figure out what direction she was going in. Even without stopping, she sometimes managed to change direction.

"We were down near Clairmont House today, and there were a lot of soldiers," said Marjorie, trying to sound very casual.

"Hush! I'm counting stitches," said Miss Agnes.

Marjorie waited until she was finished and then tried again.

"What would all those soldiers be doing at Clairmont House?"

"The army requisitioned it. I'm just surprised that it stood empty so long," said Miss Morag.

"What does that mean?" asked Anna.

"They've taken it over. The army can do that during the war—take over empty houses for soldiers to live in. I expect the officers from the army camp will make their headquarters there."

"Who did they take it over from?" asked Marjorie.

"Old Mr. Carruthers."

"But I thought he died last spring. Did he leave it to somebody?"

"The house was up for sale, but I never heard that anyone bought it. The money from the furniture mostly went to pay his debts and taxes. We all thought that he had some money hidden away, but it turned out that there wasn't so much after all. What he had mostly went on keeping up the place. Too proud to let anyone know he was down."

"Pride ruined that man's life," chimed in the other Miss Campbell.

"But what about his children?" asked Marjorie.

"There was a son killed in 1916 in the war, and then there was a daughter, much younger," said Miss Agnes.

"Losing his son in the war, and then his wife dying immediately afterwards seemed to sour the poor man," added Miss Morag. "Then he lost some of his money in the depression, but by that time it didn't matter so much. There was no one to leave it to."

"What about the daughter?" asked Marjorie.

"She had run away by then. What a scandal and gossip that caused around here! There were some that sided with him, but I felt sorry for her, poor girl," said Agnes.

"Well, it's all past and done now," said Miss Morag, her mouth closed in a prim line.

"Was the daughter called Jane?" Marjorie asked in a low voice.

"Yes, she was called Jane. Jane Carruthers," said Miss Morag. "So you've heard some of the gossip about her already. How these stories do linger on!"

"Was she pretty?" asked Anna.

"She was—beautiful," answered Miss Morag. "And it might have worked out better for everyone if she had not been quite so pretty. We used to see her walking up the road with her fine clothes and golden ringlets, all airs and graces. Much too fine for the likes of us, she was. She never spoke to us, although we were practically neighbors."

The Miss Campbells resumed their knitting, and then Miss Morag took up the story again. "There was a young artist who stayed here one winter—the winter of '27 was that? Nothing would do but what he would paint her, and he came to Clairmont House every day."

"She fell in love with him," interrupted Miss Agnes. "But her father, old Mr. Carruthers, was quite determined that Jane was going to marry money. He was beginning to worry about how he was going to keep that big house going even then, I suppose, and he wouldn't hear of her throwing herself away on a penniless artist."

"I don't think that the artist—Robert someone or other, he was—was really in love with Jane," said Morag. "I think he thought she was well off. He wasn't making much of a living with his painting. And no wonder! Do you remember that painting of his that we saw? Such a gloomy thing! Anyway, they eloped and Jane Carruthers was never seen around here again."

"That's not the end of the story," said Miss Agnes.

"The rest is just straight gossip," said Miss Morag, prim again.

Marjorie didn't know what to say. She just *had* to hear more, but was afraid to ask questions. But the Miss Campbells couldn't keep themselves from telling the rest of the story, anyway.

It was Miss Agnes who said, "They say the marriage didn't work out."

"If there was a marriage," said Miss Morag. "I've heard that when he found out that her father wasn't going to relent and let her have some money, he just left her, and she, having inherited her father's pride, never went back home."

"But there was a baby," said Miss Agnes. "Mrs. Gillespie, the chemist's wife, was up in Edinburgh and saw Jane Carruthers and she had a baby with her. Mrs. Gillespie stopped to talk to her, but Jane just turned and walked away. Still stuck up, Mrs. Gillespie said, even though her grand clothes were shabby and her hair was no longer in ringlets."

"And not long after that, we heard that she'd died," said Morag. "People here all felt that Mr. Carruthers should have tried to find the child, but they say he never did. His own grandchild and no one knows what became of it."

"Was it a boy or a girl?" asked Marjorie, her knitting quite forgotten. "And do you think maybe the father looked after it?"

"They say the father left Jane before the child was born. And as for a boy or a girl, no one seems to know. But this is just straight gossip, and we shouldn't be passing it on."

Marjorie had so much to think about that she put away her knitting and said that she wanted to go to bed early. The Miss Campbells both fussed, asking if she had a headache or was coming down with a cold.

Once in her bedroom, Marjorie pulled the painting out from under the bed and stared at it. In the corner, so obscure that it was no wonder that she had overlooked it before, she made out the tiny letters, "R.M."

Did the R stand for Robert, and the M for McInnes? Had Jane Carruthers married her artist and become Jane McInnes, and then had a daughter whom she had named Shona? Everything fit. First of all, the dates were right. And there was the picture and the fact that Shona had said that her mother came from Canonbie. There were things about Shona, herself, that fit. She didn't care too much about consequences. She got that from her mother. And she could draw—both Anna and Matron had said that she was a good artist.

Marjorie got into bed and lay for a long time, lost in romantic thoughts about poor Jane who had married her artist to escape from the lonely life she had known at Clairmont House. Then he had deserted her, leaving her with a baby and a picture of her old home. It was such a dreary picture of Clairmont House, too—much worse than it really was! Then Jane had died and the baby was sent to the orphanage, with only the painting as a clue to her past.

Just then Anna came into the bedroom, and Marjorie said, as she had been wanting to all evening, "Anna, do you realize that Jane could have been Shona's mother?"

"Your mother?" asked Anna.

"No, the real Shona's mother."

"I don't see why you say that."

"It all fits, Anna," said Marjorie. "Shona's picture of Clairmont House was painted by the artist who married Jane."

Marjorie wished that Anna would share in her excitement, but that was not Anna's way. She pulled on her nightgown and padded across the floor to switch out the light. Pretty soon her even breathing told Marjorie that she had fallen asleep, quite unconcerned about the mystery of Shona and the painting.

But Marjorie was still wide awake. She wished that she had brought the diary with her when they ran from the turret room because she wanted to read it again. Jane Carruthers had been a lonely child with no real friends and a father who shut himself away and a paid housekeeper who did not really love her. Jane was much like Marjorie herself had been in Edinburgh—a child surrounded by things, not people. How odd that she had escaped all that by changing places with Jane's daughter!

She did, however, admit that Jane's life sounded drearier than hers had been. Mrs. Kilpatrick had never locked her in her room or been cruel to her. But she had never fussed over her as the Miss Campbells did. They made her feel cared for.

She continued to think about Jane—the Jane in the diary and the Jane the Miss Campbells talked about. The lonely child and the vain, willful girl who had run away from home. If she had only heard the story from the Miss Campbells, then Shona's mother would just have been a character in a sad, romantic story. But finding the diary and hearing about her from Mrs. Appleby made her a real person who had once been a lonely little girl. She must go back and see Mrs. Appleby again, and she would ask about Becky, too.

Marjorie wondered how she could make Jane real to Shona when they met again. And what difference would it make to Shona to know? Marjorie realized that the biggest part of the discovery had been the experience of finding out, the excitement of seeing Clairmont House, and of uncovering Jane's life. How could she give that to Shona?

She drifted off to sleep thinking about it.

Several hours later Marjorie awakened suddenly, her heart beating uncomfortably hard. The sound of wailing sirens filled the whole room. It must have been the direction of the wind that night, for Marjorie had never before heard the sirens sound so loud, so urgent.

Anna stirred in her sleep and then began to cry.

"Soldiers are shooting! Soldiers are shooting us!" she shouted, sitting up in bed, pushing off her covers.

"Anna! You're dreaming," said Marjorie. "Wake up!" She tiptoed across the cold stretch of floor between the two beds and put an arm around poor, shivering Anna.

"Is that sirens?" Anna asked, shaking off the confusion of her dream, only to find the more frightening reality of an air raid.

It was during these night air raids that the war seemed close. Ration books, sweetie coupons, and empty shelves in the greengrocer's shop were an inconvenience, but that wasn't war. Even gas masks were just a bother now. On the first Monday of each month the children had to remember to take their gas masks to school to be checked, and if they forgot they were kept in. The news on the wireless was remote, and soldiers, lounging about in the town or hanging out of the back of army lorries never looked as if *they* worried about the war. But at night war was real. The sound of sirens, the throb of planes, the smells of dust and polish in the broom closet. . . .

Miss Agnes came bursting into the bedroom urging them to hurry down to the shelter. They had begun using it again. There were several troop camps in the area now, and the Canonbie people had lost their complacency when, one night, bombs had fallen only a few miles away. Billy Wallace had cycled over to see the crater. "A hole as big as a house," he told Marjorie with some relish. "Right in the middle of a field of cows."

Anna still didn't like the shelter, but tonight she crowded in beside Miss Agnes.

"Will it last long?" Anna asked.

"Maybe an hour," answered Miss Agnes.

"No, I mean the war," said Anna.

"There's no telling about that," said Miss Morag. "It might go on for years."

Years, thought Marjorie. Years before she could tell Shona about Jane Carruthers and Clairmont House. Years before she could find Marjorie Malcolm-Scott.

Chapter Twelve

❧

Although Marjorie did not realize it at the time, that morning in March when she took the Qualifying Exam was to change her life almost as much as changing places with Shona in Waverley Station the September before.

She passed the exam with flying colors and was admitted to Nettleton Academy, twelve miles from Canonbie. For the next five years she caught the bus every school morning at eight o'clock and returned home at five in the evening. Isobel McKay had passed the exam, too, so the girls traveled together and continued to be friends.

During her first year at the academy, Marjorie was no longer able to shut out news of the war. The evacuation of Dunkirk in June was followed by frightened talk of invasion. There were terrible tales of the blitz in the south. Long convoys of army lorries passed the house on their way to the army camp outside Canonbie, and occasionally tanks rumbled down the road, rattling dishes on the sideboard. The Miss Campbells worked long hours at the Canteen, serving mugs of tea and thick sandwiches to tired soldiers on the troop trains. And Marjorie and Anna continued to knit khaki scarves and squares.

There were times during the next year when Marjorie envied Shona and wished that *she* had gone to Canada, which sounded a safer, happier place to be. But gradually the far-off days "before the war" became unreal, and for long stretches of time she never thought about Mrs. Kilpatrick or Uncle Fergus or even the real Shona. "After the war" was a time that people talked about, but no longer believed in. Marjorie began to live completely in the present, worrying only about such things as homework and school friends and sweetie coupons and pocket money. She couldn't imagine what it would be like not to live with the Miss Campbells and Anna. They had become a family.

Marjorie worked very hard at school and always brought home good report cards, and the Miss Campbells were very proud when they read the glowing remarks her teachers wrote.

"Perhaps some day you'll go to the University in Edinburgh," said Miss Morag. "Quite a step up from going back to the orphanage!"

Because food was scarce, the Miss Campbells dug up their neat front lawn and planted potatoes, and when the egg ration fell to one egg a week, they decided to keep hens. Anna was delighted at this and went with Miss Morag over to see Mrs. Appleby at Escrigg Farm. They brought back a broody hen (whom Anna called Jenny) and twelve eggs for Jenny to sit on. Jenny had such a voracious appetite that the Miss Campbells wondered if they would ever come out ahead. But when the chickens finally hatched, Anna was so excited that they decided that it was all worthwhile.

One year the summer holidays were shortened to three weeks, and then school closed again in late September and early October for three more weeks so that school children could help with the potato harvest. The farm workers were all off fighting or working in munitions factories. At first Anna and Marjorie enjoyed it, but it turned out to be such hard work that they were glad when school started again.

Anna had continued to go to school in Canonbie and had made her own friends there, but her happiest hours were spent helping the Miss Campbells in the shop. The Miss Campbells often said that they didn't know how they had ever managed without her, although there was not so much business now that clothes were rationed. However, people did eventually have to replace outgrown or worn-out garments and often bought ribbons or fancy buttons to give a new look to clothes they had grown tired of.

When Anna was fourteen, she left school and went to work in the shop full time. By this time Marjorie was sixteen and had decided that she wanted to be a doctor. Although she could never have explained it to anyone, the decision was somehow tied in with Anna. There were ways in which Anna was really smart, but most people overlooked them, and Anna hadn't learned a thing in all those years at school. If Marjorie had told people about wanting to help kids like Anna, they would have said that she should become a teacher, but that wasn't Marjorie's answer. She wanted to understand Anna's problems, to know what made her different. But at sixteen you can't tell people all your ambitions. Becoming a doctor was just the first step.

When the Miss Campbells learned of her plans, they were delighted. "But the question is, how am I going to pay for it?" Marjorie asked in worried tones.

"You'll get a government grant," Miss Morag assured her. "Being an orphan, you're entitled to the maximum. And you know that Agnes and I will be glad to give you money for extras."

"So proud of you, we'll be!" said Miss Agnes, looking up at Marjorie fondly. Marjorie was tall now and not as slim as she'd like to be. Six years of starchy food and living with Miss Morag who could not abide picky eaters had done that. Her hair was light brown and she wore it curled under in a pageboy. She didn't look in the least like the dirty, woebegone child with the extraordinary haircut who had been assigned to Miss Agnes in the church hall so long ago.

So, in March of 1945, Marjorie took her Higher Learning Certificate exams and applied to Edinburgh University to study medicine.

And in May of 1945 the war ended. There were victory parades, street dances, and bonfires on every hilltop in Britain, and Marjorie thought that she must be the only person in the whole country who was not completely happy.

In actual fact, there were thousands of people who shared Marjorie's uncertainty about the future. Soldiers had to find civilian jobs, women lost their work in factories and offices, children had to learn to get along with fathers they hardly knew, and evacuees returned to homes they scarcely remembered.

The Miss Campbells had no trouble getting permission to become guardians of Anna and Marjorie. Marjorie had just turned seventeen, so there was no question of her going back to the orphanage. But she did worry about what could happen to her plans for the future when Shona came home. She had sat all those exams using someone else's name. Worse still, she had applied for a grant, claiming that she was a penniless orphan while she really had a rich uncle to support her and probably quite a lot of money of her own.

All that summer the question of her true identity weighed heavily on her mind. She felt depressed when she listened to the Miss Campbells bragging about her, but she could not bring herself to tell them what was worrying her. She felt that she had cheated them for six years.

She wondered, too, what she would tell Shona when they met. She had not thought about how they had found Clairmont House or about Jane Carruthers for ages and wondered if it had all been their romantic imaginations. How old had she been then? Eleven?

One afternoon, she went up to her bedroom, reached far under the bed, and dragged out the picture of Clairmont House. She sat for a long time gazing at it, thinking more about young Shona, who had treasured the painting, than about the picture itself. How had she got along with Uncle Fergus's cousin and her family? It must have been a terrible strain for Shona, who had grown up in an orphanage, to find herself suddenly surrounded by relatives she didn't know, who wanted to hear all about relatives she was supposed to know!

Marjorie wished that Shona could have been with them when they discovered the turret room. Then she remembered the diary. If only she had taken it so that she had something to give Shona when they met. Perhaps it was still there, lying unnoticed in the toy cupboard. She would go and find out.

Marjorie pushed the painting back under the bed and ran downstairs and outside. She hadn't been past Clairmont House for a long time, but she knew that the house was unoccupied now, because the soldiers had moved out. She was not sure, however, that she would have the nerve to go inside. She walked down the road telling herself that she would, at least, look at it one more time.

When she got there, she paused at the gate and then stared in astonishment. She was looking at the Clairmont House of the picture. The gates hung open, bent and rusted, and the huge stone gateposts leaned at drunken angles. They must have been hit, many times, by carelessly driven army lorries, and the stone ball from the top of one lay on the grass. It was just a chipped stone ball, not a skull, but she thought that perhaps if the shadows were different, the chips might look like eye sockets. The grass was long, the flower borders over-grown with rank weeds, and the shrubbery an impenetrable jungle of brambles and nettles. The house itself looked empty and forbidding. One upstairs window was broken and in another the glass was replaced with raw boards.

How could Robert McInnes have known when he painted the picture that it would, one day, look like this? It was as if he had been able to see into the future, as if he had stepped outside time. . . .

The thought overwhelmed her, and she decided that she wouldn't go inside the house after all. She would go home. As she turned to go, Dr. Knight's car stopped beside her.

"The Miss Campbells tell me you want to be a doctor, Shona," he said, his friendly eyes twinkling behind his thick-lensed glasses. He was a bewhiskered old man now, and Marjorie was fond of him.

"I leave for Edinburgh next week," she said.

"A first rate place to study," he told her. "I went there myself. But what are you doing here?"

"I was just out for a walk. We used to play here," said Marjorie.

"A friend of mine is thinking of buying this place as an old people's home and he wanted me to look it over," said Dr. Knight. "I'm sure it's hopeless—all these big, drafty rooms and stairs—but would you like to come inside with me and have a look around?"

"Oh, yes!" said Marjorie eagerly.

Dr. Knight had a key so, for the first time, Marjorie entered by the front door. They went through the house, and Dr. Knight sighed and shook his head as he went into each room. The floors were scarred from hobnailed boots, the woodwork burned with discarded cigarettes, and the whole place was in a sad state of dirt and confusion.

"We may as well go, Shona. This place would never be suitable. Goodness knows what will become of it."

"There's one more place we haven't been," said Marjorie shyly. "The little turret room."

"How do you know about that?"

"Anna and I were in here a couple of times—before the soldiers took it over."

As they walked through the hall and up the stairs, she told him about Anna's running away and about the day the soldiers nearly caught them.

"You two young girls must have led the Miss Campbells quite a dance," said Dr. Knight, his eyes twinkling again.

"I'm afraid we did," said Marjorie.

They had reached the turret room, and Marjorie

pushed the door open eagerly only to find that the room was practically bare. She gazed around, overcome with feelings of anger and disappointment. The empty cupboard, the carpet, and the curtains were still there, but the little desk and chair, the couch, the toys and books were all gone. And there was no sign of the diary.

"You should have seen it. It was such a perfect little room," said Marjorie sadly, her eyes brimming with tears.

"The war destroyed a lot of things, Shona," said Dr. Knight soberly. "But sometimes I think some good things came out of the war, too. Look how much you and Anna have done for Agnes and Morag Campbell."

"What do you mean?" asked Marjorie. "The Miss Campbells have done everything for us, not the other way around."

"Not at all," said Dr. Knight. "You girls brought a whole new interest into their lives. Before you came they were two fussy, self-centered, middle-aged ladies. They were always coming to see me with odd ailments —most of them imaginary. After you two came I've scarcely seen them. More girls like you scattered around, and my practice wouldn't be worth a darn!"

"You wouldn't say things like that—not if you really knew me!" Marjorie burst out. "You see, I'm not Shona McInnes. I've been cheating everyone all these years."

Dr. Knight looked surprised but said nothing, and Marjorie launched into the story of her long deception. When she finished, Dr. Knight crossed the room to the window seat and sat down, patting the seat beside him. "Sit down here, my dear," he said. "We'll take all that over again—slowly."

Dr. Knight listened to the story once again, shaking his head from time to time.

"And you've never heard a word from this Marjorie whoever?" he asked. "Not even now with the war over?"

"I don't see how she'd know where to write," answered Marjorie.

"I expect she could find you through the orphanage records if she wanted to. But why should she want to?"

"So that she could be herself again, I suppose," said Marjorie slowly. "I was the one who suggested it, you know. And what will happen to me when they discover I took all the exams under the wrong name and applied for a grant when I really do have money?"

"It seems to me that the other girl has the money," said Dr. Knight, shaking his head. "What I want to know is, do *you* want to change back? Do you want to find your Uncle Fergus again?"

Marjorie shook her head. "I think of the Miss Campbells and Anna as my family now. And I really *do* want to be a doctor, and I don't think that's the sort of thing Uncle Fergus would have wanted for his niece. His friends' daughters went to boarding schools and finishing schools, though I suppose the war has ended some of that. But I *do* want to be something useful, Dr. Knight, and I'm so worried about what will happen when people find out."

"You leave it to me," said Dr. Knight. "I'll vouch for your character. But, you know, I do think that when you go to Edinburgh you've got to try and find this Marjorie person. For your own sake and for hers. You should both face up to what you did, but as I see it, that's for the two of you to work out. Now, let's get along home. It's almost time for evening surgery."

Chapter Thirteen

~

The Miss Campbells and Anna went with Marjorie to Canonbie Station to see her off on the Edinburgh train. Marjorie looked at these people who had become her family and suddenly remembered timid little Anna Ray in the railway station six years before and the fussy, identical twin sisters who had taken them in. How they had all changed, she thought. They hadn't just grown six years older. They had become different people, and that was partly because they had known each other. She must be different, too.

A boy, who had been in Anna's class at school and now worked for the railway, shouted something to Anna, and she grinned at him, tossing back her dark, shoulder-length hair. She was pretty now, and although she was still quiet, she wasn't as shy as she used to be.

The Miss Campbells were both wearing their tweed coats, but they no longer dressed exactly alike. That dated right back to the day that Anna burned Miss Agnes's best silk dress. Today, Miss Morag was wearing a green felt hat and Miss Agnes had a bright scarf knotted around her head. Wisps of hair straggled out from under it, and she looked younger than her sister as she handed Marjorie a small package.

"Just something to nibble on in the train, my dear," she said, and then looked as if she were going to break down and cry.

"Now it won't be long until Christmas," said Miss Morag firmly. "And think how much Shona will have to tell us."

Marjorie turned away and stared down the track. In the distance she could see a puff of smoke. The train was coming, and neither the Miss Campbells nor Anna could possibly have guessed the depth of Marjorie's feelings as she watched the train approaching along the straight stretch of track.

It was coming to take the Shona McInnes that they had known back to Edinburgh, where her new life had started six years before. She had the frightened feeling that nothing would ever be the same again. Suddenly she wanted to stay safe in Canonbie, hidden away from the real Shona.

But the train came on, whistling and thundering, and screeched to a halt.

"All aboard for Edinburgh!" shouted the porter, and doors banged open and shut.

The Miss Campbells eagerly helped Marjorie lift her heavy suitcase into the train—so much bigger than the little cardboard case that she had carried six years before. And inside was the picture, the thread that tied her to Shona McInnes.

For the first few days in Edinburgh Marjorie was so busy that she found it easy to tell herself that there was no time to go anywhere near Willowbrae Road. She was living in a student hostel and busied herself with registration and buying books and finding her way to lectures. But every time she wrote the name, Shona McInnes—as she did repeatedly during these first few days on forms, on registration cards, in new text books —the uncertain feeling of not quite knowing who she was came nagging back.

On Saturday morning Marjorie lingered over breakfast, then tidied her room, and wrote a long letter to the Miss Campbells. At last, she knew she couldn't put it off any longer, so she pulled on her coat and went out.

It was a bright, clear day, but there was a cold wind from the east, and Marjorie turned up the collar of her coat and shoved her hands into her pockets, as she stood at the tram stop waiting for a Number Eight tram car to Portobello. When the tram came, she climbed inside and took a seat next to the window. Could she still find her way back to the house on Willowbrae Road? Beyond that, she dared not think.

The tram car rattled around a curve, and she recognized a massive church ahead of her, its stone walls stained black with age. How many times had she and Mrs. Kilpatrick got off the tram just here on their way back from a shopping excursion to Princes Street, she wondered. She rose from her seat as in a dream, stepped down from the tram, walked past the shops, and then turned up the long hill that led to Willowbrae Road.

She counted off the houses, her heart beating uncomfortably loud, and then found herself, at last, standing in front of her own familiar house. The curtains were closed, and a feeling of relief swept through her because she was sure that the house was empty. Just the same, she pushed open the little wrought-iron gate and walked up the path and rang the bell. No one answered.

Marjorie walked slowly away from the house toward the narrow gate that led into Holyrood Park. She followed the road through the park down to the little pond where the orphanage children used to play. A group of children were feeding the ducks, and Marjorie half expected to see a small, fair-haired girl in a faded, red coat among them.

She sat down on a park bench. Inside her head she could hear her own anxious voice asking, "But how will we change back?" Shona had answered, "I'll work that out. After the war—in Holyrood Park." But it was more complicated now than just switching clothes. She looked down at her brown winter coat. The Miss Campbells had sacrificed some of their clothing coupons to help her buy a new coat for coming to Edinburgh. She couldn't give that away!

With a sigh, Marjorie got up and walked back to the tram stop. Somehow she had to contact Shona, and the only way she could think of doing that was to start from the house on Willowbrae Road. She went back to the house twice more, and each time it was empty. The first time Marjorie was relieved, but the second time she felt depressed. The uncertainty of the future was gnawing at her. It would soon be the end of term, and she somehow felt that she could not go back to Canonbie and the Miss Campbells without making a greater effort to find Shona. There must be something else she could do.

One Saturday in December, she decided to try the house one more time, but at the last minute she took a tram to Princes Street instead. The shops were very crowded, and on a sudden impulse, looking for somewhere quiet, she turned into a small art gallery just off Princes Street. There was a showing of paintings by war artists in one room, which did not greatly interest her, but nevertheless, she went in and looked casually at the stark and awful paintings.

Suddenly her attention was riveted to the work of one artist. The first painting was of a plane, wrecked in a desert. Pieces of distorted metal lay half buried in the sand. One piece, bent and twisted, cast a shadow like a swastika, and another—a huge lump of metal—was highlighted so that it looked like a skull. Marjorie walked toward the painting to examine it more closely and peering at the right-hand corner saw, as she had been sure she would, the small letters, "R.M."

There were several other paintings signed "R.M." One was of pipes, twisted together, a meaningless thing. She turned away and went back out to the reception desk and asked an old man if he could tell her the names of the artists in the war pictures exhibit.

"Didn't ye get a paper as ye went in, lass?" he asked her. "It tells a bit about each o' them."

Marjorie snatched the paper from his hand and ran her eye down the sheet.

There it was! Robert McInnes. 1903–1943.

This was followed by a brief biography: "Robert McInnes was employed as a war artist to make sketches of enemy installations in places where photography was impossible. His sketches were of little use to the Government because he sacrificed accuracy for emotional impact. However, his paintings are likely to have lasting value as a graphic interpretation of scenes of the war. He was killed in active duty in November, 1943."

"Paintings of lasting value." Here, at last, was something she could give to Shona. The father whom she had never known had left something so that people would remember him. Surely, through his paintings, Shona could find out about him herself.

Clutching the flimsy paper, Marjorie turned and walked out of the gallery and caught a tram toward Willowbrae Road. When she reached the house, she was, somehow, not surprised to see that today the curtains were open and the house was lived in.

She walked up to the door and rang the bell. She listened to the slow tread of answering footsteps. The door opened, and there stood Mrs. Kilpatrick looking at her stolidly.

Marjorie just stood there, waiting for the spate of words that would surely come when Mrs. Kilpatrick recognized her. Mrs. Kilpatrick looked so much the same to Marjorie that it seemed inconceivable to Marjorie that Mrs. Kilpatrick would not know *her*. But Marjorie was quite changed from the little blond pig-tailed girl who had lived there six years before, the girl who had worn tailored coats and black patent leather shoes. Marjorie's winter coat was new but was, after all, just a plain, wartime coat. She wore flat brown shoes and thick lisle stockings. She'd grown tall, and her hair, now brown, was curled—somewhat limp and straggly curls on that raw December afternoon.

When the silence became uncomfortably long, Mrs. Kilpatrick asked sharply, "Well, what can I do for you?"

"Is Marjorie Malcolm-Scott here?" Marjorie asked. And added by way of explanation, "We used to be friends."

"She is here. She's just back from Canada, you know. But I don't remember her having friends in the old days."

"We played together—in the park," said Marjorie in a small voice.

Mrs. Kilpatrick looked at Marjorie curiously for a minute and then said, rather grudgingly, "Come inside, and I'll call her."

She led Marjorie into the Victorian sitting room, and Marjorie looked around. Everything in the room was just as she remembered it, even the seven ebony elephants arranged on the mantelpiece. It was all so familiar, yet all so strange.

"What name shall I say?" asked Mrs. Kilpatrick.

Marjorie gave a start and then said, "Shona McInnes. She'll know who it is."

Mrs. Kilpatrick bustled out and came back in a few minutes.

"She says she'll be down. Please take a seat."

Marjorie sat down feeling dreadfully nervous.

"How long has she been back?" she asked.

"Just a week—and she's not back to stay. Her Uncle Fergus wanted to see her, so she came over for Christmas, but she plans to go back to her relatives in Canada. And I can understand it. She's more at home there."

"And her Uncle doesn't mind?"

"I think he was relieved at first that she had decided to live in Canada, but now, I don't know. Such a smart and pretty girl she's turned out. Her Uncle said that he wouldn't have recognized her when he met her off the boat if she hadn't sent us her photograph. She's not the quiet, sulky little thing she used to be before the war."

Marjorie bristled at that and felt some of her nervousness leave her. The door opened and a tall, slim girl wearing a gray skirt, pale blue twin set, and silk stockings stepped into the room. She tossed back her golden hair and said almost imperiously, "You can leave us, Mrs. Kilpatrick!" She spoke with a Canadian accent.

Marjorie stood up and wondered what to say, but Shona spoke first, saying, "Mrs. Kilpatrick says that your name is Shona McInnes. I'm afraid I don't remember you."

She stared at Marjorie with a cold, calculating gleam in her blue eyes.

"Of course, you do," stuttered Marjorie. "The day in Waverley Station when we changed places."

"I don't know what you're talking about."

"I've found out about your family," said Marjorie nervously. "Look, if you don't want to change back, it's all right with me, but we've got to talk about it."

"I'm afraid there's nothing to talk about."

"Don't you at least want to know about your mother and father? I was sent to Canonbie. I felt awful at first because you should have been the one to go there, and you would have found Clairmont House for yourself. It would have meant more to you. The house in the picture, you know."

Marjorie knew she wasn't putting it well, but Shona's icy stare unnerved her.

"I know all there is to know about my parents," said Shona in a low, steady voice. "They were drowned in a yachting accident when I was five. I'm Marjorie Malcolm-Scott, and immediately after Christmas I'm going back to live with my cousins in Canada, and I doubt if I'll ever come back here."

Then she added, very slowly, looking directly at Marjorie, "And there's no way you can change that."

"But can't I tell you about your parents?" begged Marjorie. "I thought you used to wonder about them. Look, you should at least go to this art gallery."

She thrust the flimsy paper she was still holding into Shona's hand. Without even glancing at it, Shona crumpled it up and hurled it into the fire, and they both watched it burn.

Just then the door opened and a tall, slightly stooped, gray-haired man walked into the room. Uncle Fergus! Marjorie looked at him expectantly, but his glance just slid off her, almost as if she was not there. He turned to Shona and said, "I didn't know you had company, Marjorie."

"She's just leaving," said Shona smoothly. "I'll ring for Mrs. Kilpatrick to show her out."

"I'll show myself out," said Marjorie, and added to Shona as she walked between her and Uncle Fergus, "After all, I know the way!"

She left the house, slamming the door behind her. Shona's voice was still ringing in her ears. *I'm Marjorie Malcolm-Scott, and there's no way you can change that!* She could see the hard look on Shona's face, and for a moment she felt strangely sorry for her. Yes, Shona could keep her money, her relatives, and even her name! Marjorie walked down Willowbrae Road feeling bold, confident, and daring. She had found herself at last. And she liked what she had found.

MARGARET J. ANDERSON, a native of Scotland, was graduated from the University of Edinburgh with honors in genetics. Since then she has worked as a biologist, a statistician, and a writer in England, Canada, and the United States. She is the author of many fantasy novels for young readers, including the award-winning *In the Circle of Time* and, her most recent book, *The Druid's Gift*.

Ms. Anderson lives in Corvallis, Oregon, with her husband and four children.